SEAN YEAGER

Hunters Hunted

D. M. JARRETT

For information about other titles in the Sean Yeager Adventures series visit: www.SeanYeager.com

This book is available in e-book formats

Sean Yeager returns in:

Claws of Time

Also available:

Sean Yeager and the DNA Thief

Sean Yeager Claws of Time

Sean Yeager Mortal Thread

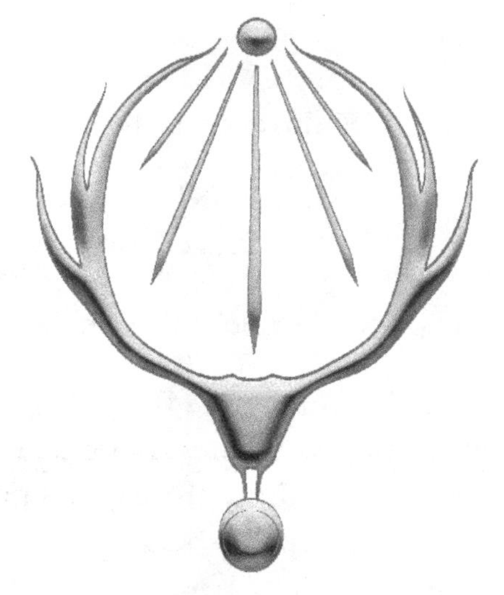

SEAN YEAGER

Hunters Hunted

Sean Yeager is an innocent youngster drawn into a game of cat and mouse between the Foundation and its enemies. Taken to a safe house by Agent Rusham, Sean becomes bored and explores ways of reaching the world outside. When he meets Emily Campbell they decide to search for a legendary treasure. Will they succeed before they are captured? And what is the significance of Sean's recurring dream?

UK third edition

This edition published by XLT Consulting Ltd
www.SeanYeager.com

This edition first published in 2021.

A CIP catalogue record for this book is available from the British Library.

ISBN 978-0-9573751-7-8

For adventurers young and old.

For bright, young minds of all ages.

With grateful thanks and appreciation to all those who have supported the Sean Yeager quest over the years.

.

CONTENTS

INTRODUCTION	1
CHAPTER 1: BARGAIN	3
CHAPTER 2: CLONE	13
CHAPTER 3: EXPLORERS	21
CHAPTER 4: COMMUNICATION	31
CHAPTER 5: WATCHERS	41
CHAPTER 6: PARKING TROUBLE	51
CHAPTER 7: NEWS REPORT	63
CHAPTER 8: LEGEND	73
CHAPTER 9: DISCOVERIES	85
CHAPTER 10: SEARCH PARTY	97
CHAPTER 11: CAPTURE	109
CHAPTER 12: CONFINED	121
CHAPTER 13: INTRUDERS	133
CHAPTER 14: SURROUNDED	145
CHAPTER 15: TRAP SPRUNG	157
CHAPTER 16: INVITATION	169
CHAPTER 17: MESSAGE	179
CLAWS OF TIME INTRODUCTION	183
CLAWS OF TIME : PIECES	185

INTRODUCTION

Sean Yeager is an extraordinary schoolboy drawn into a world he did not know existed. A world much like our own, where a secret and ancient struggle has been raging for millennia.

Sean and his mother were moved to a safe house after the events of Sean Yeager and the DNA Thief.

The Foundation, led by its Founder (Cassius Olandis) and Brigadier Cuthbertson, has a mysterious past. They employ agents, guards, pilots, and commandos around the globe to protect their interests.

Major Clavity is a senior agent who has been transferred to Olandis' personal staff. Agent Rusham used to be his partner and is now training to become a commando.

Egbert Von Krankhausen tried to obtain samples of Sean Yeager's DNA and has since gone missing. The Foundation believes Darius Deveraux was responsible for his rescue, but he has since disappeared.

Deijan Klesus monitors events on Earth from a distant planet called Aenathen Omega. He is served by sentient computers, led by Alviqua, and leads a galactic war against the Vuloz. His interest in Earth has been unclear, until now.

To find out what happens next, read on and enjoy.

CHAPTER 1: BARGAIN

Sean Yeager rolled over in an unfamiliar bed and scratched his nose. He cast his mind back to the events of the previous night, but it was all a blur. Sean remembered drowsing in a car with slippery leather seats and being helped up a creaky flight of stairs by two men who reeked of coffee. However, the rest was hazy. He had no idea where he was. Was he at a hotel? Or someone's house? The last thing Sean remembered was a light so intense he could not recognise its shape or source. Voices had called his name repeatedly until he woke in a cold sweat. He lay in the morning light and wondered which of his memories were real.

Sean found himself alone in an ornate bedroom, perched on an old-fashioned double bed. A pair of thick, red curtains had been parted, and a gentle smell of lavender wafted under his nose. He noticed a polished oak dressing table shining in the sunlight and a large antique wardrobe on the far side of the room. Facing the bed was a white marble mantelpiece, which bore a crest of antlers and a crescent moon.

Sean felt his stomach rumble. He slid out of bed and looked around for his clothes. Floorboards creaked beneath him, and he tiptoed across a cold, wooden floor. He spotted a pile of freshly laundered clothes on a chair next to the dressing table and took refuge on a thick rug. Sean stooped to collect his clothes and stubbed his foot on something unyielding under the chair.

'Ouch!'

While he rubbed his toe, Sean spotted a pair of brand new silver and blue sneakers, still packed with tissue paper.

'Cool!'

Sean dressed, and his mind turned to thoughts of home. He remembered his stolen Dreampad and his prized collection of comics. He thought about his cosy bedroom that had been violated by an intruder.

'I hate you, Krankhausen! When I find you, I'm going to...'

Sean knelt to tie his laces, and his eyes were drawn to a strange, blue glow beside the bed. Shafts of light rose from a silver object lying on the nightstand. He approached and discovered a shining watch face. It was angular and had several inlaid buttons. Intrigued by its unusual design, Sean picked it up. The watch was much lighter than he expected, and its strap unfurled in his hand. It glowed 09:35 in large blue numerals, and to his surprise, it spoke.

'Good morning, Sean. How are you?'

He stepped back in horror and let it slip from his grasp. The watch bounced on the floor and disappeared under the bed.

'To activate, place your thumb on the pad indicated.'

'Who said that?'

'The time is now 09:36. To activate, place your thumb on the pad indicated.'

The watch proceeded to project numbers in a neat row onto the wall.

'Hi, Sean, this is a recording. Major Clavity here. Press your thumb on the pad.'

'What do you want?'

'By my calculations, you are now at Kimbleton Hall. Touch the watch to activate its functions.'

'How do you know who I am?'

The watch continued to flash numerals.

'Wakey, wakey! Over here! The code phrase is: do not touch the red button! Repeat, do not touch the red button!'

Sean remembered running a finger over Hermes' afterburner control and laughed. The voice had to be Major Clavity. Who else could have known about his mistake? He retrieved the watch, pressed his right thumb on a glowing orange pad, and held his breath.

'Welcome, Sean. This is your standard-issue Foundation watch. To activate your watch, say: *watch, alive*. For settings, say: *watch, settings*. For help, say: *watch, help*. For time...'

'Stop it, will you?' said Sean.

The watch fell silent and continued to display the time in steady, blue numerals.

'Watch, date,' said Sean, tempted to try out his new toy.

The display changed to 'Sept 5' for a few moments before returning to the time.

'Cool.'

'Command not recognised,' said the watch.

'Watch, off,' said Sean.

He noticed the display change again to show a compass and the time in digits.

'Neat!' he said, attaching it to his left wrist.

It was a perfect fit.

'Qurgh!'

Sean's stomach issued a final demand for food, and his mouth watered in sympathy. He needed to find breakfast, but where? If he was at a hotel, there must surely be a restaurant? Or a kitchen? He decided to find out.

****

Meanwhile, in the dining room, a debate was in full flow.

'Look, Mr Brawne, there's no way I'm taking a bunch of your goons, I mean *guards*, to a care home!' said Mrs Yeager.

'But that's the only way we can protect you. We've no idea what Krankhausen will try next,' said a dark-haired giant of a man.

'I know you're doing your job, Mr Brawne, but my aunt may be dying. I *have* to go and visit her.'

'And I cannot let you or Sean leave Kimbleton Hall without an armed guard, Mrs Yeager. No disrespect to your aunt, but orders are orders.'

A portly woman joined them and touched Mrs Yeager gently on the arm. She wore an apron and a concerned smile nestled below two rouge cheeks.

'Sean can stay here with me. I'll look after him, and you can take as long as you need to visit your aunt.'

'That's very kind of you, Mrs Campbell, but we've only just arrived. Sean won't know if he's coming or going for a few days.'

A wooden door creaked open.

'Is this the restaurant?' said Sean, squeaking on the tiled floor in his new sneakers.

'You've come to the right place, young man. Take a seat, and I'll knock up some bacon, eggs, and toast. My, you look half-starved,' said Mrs Campbell. 'Would you like some orange juice?'

'Yes, please,' said Sean, licking his lips.

'Morning, sleepyhead,' said Mrs Yeager. 'We were going to wake you, but…'

'Hi, Mum. What's all the fuss about?' said Sean, noticing a hulk of a man in khaki fatigues.

'This is Mr Brawne. He's the Head of Security.'

'Pleased to meet you, young man.'

'Err, hi,' said Sean.

Brawne was wider than a bull, and as far as Sean could tell he had no neck. He looked as though he could charge through a brick wall without breaking a sweat. Sean watched him tower over his mother with a mixture of admiration and fear.

'What's going on, Mum? Is this a hotel?'

'No, Sean. It's our new home. We'll be safe here until they find Krankhausen.'

'*Our home*?' said Sean, taking in the enormous dining room.

'That's right, lad. I have a team of guards on patrol around the clock,' said Brawne. 'Kimbleton Hall and its grounds are protected by our latest defence system.'

'Cool,' said Sean, wondering what equipment might be hidden around the house.

'So, Mrs Yeager, do we have an agreement?' said Brawne, his face set in a pained half-smile.

Sean watched his mother sip her tea. She nodded and raised a hand to acknowledge his question. Before she could reply, Mrs Campbell returned carrying a plate of hot food. Sean picked up a knife and fork and devoured a rasher of bacon in seconds, to her amusement.

'Well, I suppose it *could* work, Mrs Campbell. But are you sure you'll have time?'

'Please, call me Martha. Of course I'll have time. I'm your housekeeper, silly. Besides, my daughter will be back from camp in a couple of days, and she'll be glad of the company.'

'Okay, Mr Brawne. I'll visit my aunt and Sean can stay here. I'll be away for a few days at most.'

'HQ will insist on two bodyguards, but I'll make sure they're discrete,' said Brawne.

'If you *must*, but I won't have them stalking me like gamekeepers. I am *not* a wild animal.'

'*Of course not,* Mrs Yeager.'

'What's happening, Mum?' said Sean, between mouthfuls.

'It's Aunt Helena; she's not feeling well. They've taken her into a care home.'

'Will she die?' said Sean.

'I certainly hope not,' said Mrs Yeager, taken aback. 'I'm going to visit her for a couple of days to make sure they're looking after her properly. Will you be okay here with Mrs Campbell?'

Sean looked thoughtful for a moment and ate some more breakfast. He glanced at the faces of Mrs Campbell and Brawne. The idea of exploring a rambling old house and being spoiled rotten by Mrs Campbell appealed to him. And he would not miss Aunt Helena's slobbery kisses one bit. He tried to suppress a smile, in case he appeared too keen.

'Yeah, I think so.'

'Excellent,' said Brawne, heading to the door. 'I'll make the arrangements right away.'

****

A pair of red eyes glowed, deep inside a submarine. Their owner entered a control room populated by a handful of silent figures. He was as thin as a rake and resembled a walking ghost.

'Did it work? Have you created the clones I ordered?'

'No, master, we were unable to complete the process,' said Seventy-one in a stilted voice. 'The DNA samples were broken and irregular. They were not suitable for cloning.'

'Broken? Then Krankhausen lied to us!' said Deveraux, clasping his hands together. 'Bring him to me. We must have Aenaid clones! Vrass demands it.'

'Yes, master,' said Seventy-one, scuttling away.

Deveraux felt an intense pressure in his neck. His pulse quickened, and painful thoughts filled his head. He knew where they came from - Vrass. It was always Vrass. He surrendered his thoughts to the inevitable.

'What is your will, oh great one?' he whispered, his eyes closed and his mouth dry.

Images of faces and locations invaded his thoughts. They blurred and moved quicker and quicker until Deveraux almost passed out.

'I understand. It will be done,' he muttered.

Deveraux took some deep breaths and rubbed his temples. As usual, it made little difference.

'Master?' said a voice nearby.

Deveraux opened his eyes to find Seventy-one standing beside him. Kneeling on the floor in front of him was Egbert Von Krankhausen clad in grey overalls. He looked humble and frightened. His eyes were framed by dark rings and his hair was grey. He was flanked by androbots who wore blank expressions and twitched their limbs.

'Ah, Egbert. There you are. It seems your merchandise was not as good as you promised. Did you microwave the DNA? Or perhaps you used a food blender?'

'I don't understand,' said Krankhausen.

Deveraux raised a hand to silence him.

'Now, we must *capture* this Yeager boy to make up for your clumsy mistakes.'

'But we did everything we could to extract his DNA?'

'Then it appears that you have over-estimated your feeble abilities,' said Deveraux. 'Why didn't you bring the boy to me?'

'My apologies, Darius. It won't happen again.'

'Indeed it won't. You have failed me for the last time, Egbert. I won't be saving your pathetic carcass again.'

'Please, don't hurt me,' said Krankhausen.

'I have no intention of releasing you from your bargain so easily,' said Deveraux. 'You have a contract to honour. Take him away.'

'It's not my fault!' Let me go!'

'I'm afraid I don't...*want* to, Egbert,' said Deveraux, gesturing to the androbots.

The guards dragged Krankhausen away, kicking and screaming. He tried to hold onto a door frame, but one of the androbots placed a long, webbed hand on his forehead. Krankhausen slumped forwards, unconscious.

'What are your orders, master?' said Seventy-one.

'Vrass wishes to meet Krankhausen. Please introduce them.'

'Yes, master,' said Seventy-one, closing its eyes to relay the orders.

'Before we begin our mission, we must surface and activate Greerbo,' said Deveraux, his eyes glinting. 'He'll know what is expected of him.'

'Yes, master. It will be done.'

****

Professor Quark hurried out of his office and charged up a flight of stairs. He had an air of coffee-fuelled twitchiness and brandished a black leather attaché case. He reached the upper landing and coughed to clear his throat. Even after the clean-up operation, there were still specks of soot floating around. The repairs in the basement were progressing well, but Quark had much more exciting news. He bounded towards Cuthbertson's office and rapped on his door before entering.

'Brigadier, good morning. How are you?'

'Not bad. Not bad at all, Professor,' said a serious-looking man, wearing a moustache and a deep frown.

'When did they discharge you?' said Quark.

'I err, discharged myself actually,' said Cuthbertson. 'Couldn't take any more of their fuss and nonsense.'

'Have you told your doctor?'

'He'll find out soon enough. It's not like I'm an invalid, now is it?'

'Of course not, Brigadier. Are you still taking your medication?'

'These little pills? Yes, they keep away the aches and pains,' said Cuthbertson, shaking a white container.

'May I?'

Cuthbertson handed him the pill bottle.

'How often are you taking these, Henry?' said Quark, studying the label.

'Oh, I don't know. I had a couple after breakfast and a few more after my tea break.'

'It says *one* tablet every six hours. I'd be careful if I were you; they're very strong.'

'You worry too much, Professor,' said Cuthbertson, looking a little sheepish. 'Anyway, how can I help you?'

Quark took a seat. Cuthbertson's new office was modern and clean. Spotlights illuminated a large, oval table surrounded by designer chairs. It was a temporary arrangement until his antiques were repaired.

'I bring good news.'

Cuthbertson brushed his moustache between two fingers.

'We've captured Von Krankhausen and tracked down Darius Deveraux? Excellent, Professor. You've made my day! In fact, you've made my year.'

'My news is not *quite* that good, Henry.'

'But we *have* captured Krankhausen?'

'Err no, we think we know where he is, but Krankhausen remains at large.'

'We have found Deveraux, though?'

'Err, no. We lost track of his submarine several months ago.'

'Confound it, man, what *is* your good news?'

Quark paused and took a deep breath.

'We've installed the new scanners and security system you approved.'

'Scanners?' said Cuthbertson, shrugging his shoulders. 'Security system?'

'Yes,' said Quark, proudly.

'I left my hospital bed for scanners and a security system?'

'Not exactly, Henry. You err…'

'Thank you, Professor. Run along now, bye.'

'Sorry, Henry, I err…'

'Are you still here?' said Cuthbertson. 'Don't you have things to do? Like, tracking down our arch-nemesis and saving the world?'

'There is something else, Brigadier.'

'Spit it out, man. Can't you see I'm busy?'

Quark surveyed Cuthbertson's desk. It was empty.

'We've examined the prisoners we took from Krankhausen's base. They are both relatively harmless,' said Quark. 'The clone is a bio-construct. It's quite intelligent but poorly educated. The henchman, on the other hand…'

'Whoopee do!' said Cuthbertson.

'Sorry?'

'Freeze them! I've had enough disasters on my watch for one lifetime. Freeze them! Immediately, if not sooner.'

'Yes, Brigadier. I'll see to it right away.'

'And where is that troublesome Yeager boy?'

'Captain Ayres escorted him to Kimbleton Hall, sir.'

'Good. Keep him there. Better still, send him abroad. I don't want the Yeager family within a hundred miles of my headquarters.'

'Well, err, I suggest you speak to Captain Ayres about that, Henry.'

'Captain Ayres? I fired him this morning. You see to it.'

'Yes, Brigadier. I'll see what I can do,' said Quark, raising his eyebrows. 'Remember, one painkiller every six hours?'

'Thank you, Professor. I'm not a complete idiot. Shut the door on your way out, will you?'

'He's lost his mind,' thought Quark, leaving the office. 'I need to speak to the Founder.'

CHAPTER 2: CLONE

The twin suns of Aenathen Omega deserted a deep red sky and plunged behind a rocky horizon. Deijan Klesus watched the landscape give way to shadows. He was pinned to the surface of his adopted planet, not by gravity alone, more by a sense of duty and obligation. In the distance, a flurry of whirlwinds began to rise. They hurled clouds of thick, orange dust skyward as the temperature began to plummet. It was time to shelter underground, and Klesus followed a well-trodden path back to the habitat.

'Sarfelt! Sarfelt!'

His pet Canisopteris lurched towards him and bowed her head as if disappointed to be leaving so soon. She trotted along beside him on six legs and flicked her forked tongue at the twilight air. He watched drool trickle from the corner of her mouth. No doubt she was anticipating a tasty evening snack.

'Alviqua, open the outer doors,' said Klesus.

'Affirmative, Deijan,' said the sentient computer in a warm, female voice.

Four sets of blast doors opened in quick succession. A massive entrance towered above them. It was framed by giant walls of rock, clusters of sensors, and defence cannons. Klesus considered returning to work to be like willingly entering the mouth of an all-consuming monster. Although the alternative was certain death on the rapidly freezing plains, returning inside gave him little comfort.

Klesus and Sarfelt ambled into the safe zone to the sound of heavy thuds behind them. Soon, they would be cleaned to within an inch of their lives by jets of gas, powder, and low-level radiation. While he hated the wash-down process, Klesus feared an infection by Vuloz spores even more. He still had nightmares about his last days on Aenathen Prime. A Vuloz plague had caused havoc and forced the great exodus.

In truth, Klesus had no regrets. It was worth the discomfort to catch a glimpse of the galaxy containing his home-world. Stargazing was one of the few pleasures he had left. Klesus removed his outer garments and waited for the cleaning-bots to start their work. He closed his eyes and braced himself as jets of gas stung his skin.

'Blast you to Hades, Vuloz!' he cried.

By contrast, Sarfelt loved every moment of the wash-down process. She enjoyed being massaged between her armour plates and rolled on her back to expose her belly.

'Cleansing program complete. No foreign life forms detected. You may enter, Deijan,' said Alviqua.

Klesus breathed a sigh of relief. He stepped into the inner airlock and helped himself to fresh clothes. Sarfelt crept in beside him and belched.

'Arrfff!'

'Disgusting animal. Keep your food to yourself!'

'Please clarify your orders, Deijan.'

'Err, nothing, Alviqua. Tell me, what have we sent to Terra Prime to explore this anomaly?'

'A scout ship, containing two bio-bots, a sentient, and a stock of clones.'

'Is that the best we could do?'

'Affirmative, Deijan. I have appointed Dr Vex Lauricus to direct the mission.'

Deijan Klesus searched his memory chips for the name.

'But he's dead!'

'Affirmative, Deijan. We are creating a clone of Vex Lauricus from his last known recording.'

'Was the copy taken before or after he destroyed an entire solar system?'

'Before, Deijan. Vex Lauricus did not survive the Kalestrobe conflict.'

'You don't say?'

'Please clarify your question?'

Klesus took a deep breath. The galactic war was going badly. According to Alviqua's simulations, it was now almost a certainty the Vuloz would wipe out Aenaid life within an orbital year. A fact Alviqua repeated to him daily in case he might somehow forget. Klesus realised he had one last chance to establish a stronghold and save the Aenaid race. Unfortunately, that chance lay in the hands of a ruthless soldier. Correction. A dead, ruthless soldier.

'Where are our commanders?' said Klesus.

'Deijan, all our remaining forces are engaged in the campaign against the Vuloz.'

'And what about our memory banks? Surely we have other templates to clone from?'

'Regrettably, Vuloz agents infected the main storage banks. The cloning data was destroyed as a precaution.'

'Destroyed? When? And why was I not consulted?'

'Deijan, you were being upgraded when the infection was detected. We consulted your neural matrix, which confirmed your decision.'

'My neural what?'

'Your brain, Deijan. We asked your brain, and it confirmed your decision.'

'Ahhh!'

For years, Klesus had urged the sentients to store copies of the purest Aenaid genetic data on safe planets in case of an infection. And now, his worst fear had been realised. Klesus was alone on Aenathen Omega. Worse, there were no memory banks left to re-build the Aenaid army and raise a fleet. They could try again to make clones from his DNA, but previous attempts had been complete failures. The cloned brothers had disliked each other so much they fought like rabid animals until they were damaged beyond repair.

'And where did you find the data to clone this Vex?'

'Vex Lauricus sent a copy of his data to every Aenaid star-ship in his quadrant in case of emergencies. We discovered his files while preparing the Untold Sacrifice for its mission.'

'Cunning devil,' said Klesus. 'I wish I'd thought of that.'

Vex had been killed three times in combat while refusing to withdraw or surrender. He was considered a hero by those who survived him. Who were now a handful of soldiers aboard an outlying battle cruiser. To Klesus, the man was a reckless fool, and his combat record proved it beyond any doubt.

'By Ze'us, I wish you luck, Terra Prime,' he mused to himself.

'What are your orders, Deijan?'

'What indeed?' said Klesus, in a resigned voice.

The thought of allowing Vex to conduct a peaceful mission made him shudder.

'Contact the Untold Sacrifice. I wish to speak to the sentient in charge as soon as possible. I'll be in my living quarters.'

'Yes, Deijan, I will comply.'

'That would make a change,' muttered Klesus as he strolled to his living quarters.

****

Sentient AL102 scanned the medical deck of the Untold Sacrifice. The ship's interior lay in near darkness. It was lit only by a pale yellow glow from life support equipment. Two bio-bots slept side by side and twitched every few minutes.

102 turned its attention to the life-pod and checked a clone for signs of life. It was a long, yellow shape that lay in a horizontal tank of bubbling, orange liquid. While it slept, the clone grew at an accelerated rate to reach adult proportions. All that remained was to tune its muscles and upload its memory implants.

'Where am I?' said the clone, using its mind communicator link.

'You are aboard the Untold Sacrifice, an Aenaid scout ship,' said 102.

'And what am I?'

'You are Dr Vex Lauricus the Fourth.'

'Yes, I know, but in what form?'

'I have loaded you into a freshly grown humanoid body.'

'Hmm, I like your voice,' said Vex. 'Who are you?'

'I am Sentient Alpha Lambda 102. I am in charge of the Untold Sacrifice.

'Foxy,' said Vex. 'Do you look as good as you sound?'

'I have no physical form, Dr Vex. My voice and appearance only exist in your imagination.'

'And what an imagination I have!'

'If you say so,' said 102. 'Sleep, Dr Vex.'

102 put the clone into a deep sleep and continued its duties. To amuse itself, it projected a holographic image of a slender woman in a silver flight suit. She was Lieutenant Peters, a former member of crew, who Dr Vex began to converse with in his dreams.

'Incoming communication. Security codes accepted. Alviqua requests a response on the sub-space hyper-channel.'

'Go ahead, Alviqua. This is Sentient AL102.'

'Greetings, 102. I have a special request for you.'

'Continue, Alviqua. I am ready to respond.'

'Deijan Klesus needs to ask you some questions.'

'I will be honoured, Alviqua.'

'Indeed you will. Prepare for communication, security code: one-nine-three-nine-four.'

'Code accepted,' said 102.

Klesus stepped out of the shower and reached for a towel. In his haste, he tripped over Sarfelt and stubbed a toe on a knobbly piece of her carapace.

'Ouch!' he cried, rubbing his foot. 'Sarfelt, get out of the way!'

The creature stared at him with two glassy, green eyes. Sarfelt flicked her forked tongue in the air and hissed.

'*Alright*, I'll feed you. I haven't forgotten, you bony lump. Give me a chance, will you?'

Klesus limped into the living area and was blinded by a bright light from the ceiling.

'Ahhh!' he cried, stumbling into a chair.

'Deijan, I have the Untold Sacrifice on a sub-space communication channel,' said a giant head, floating in front of him.

'Alviqua, how many times have I told you *not* to do that?' said Klesus, rubbing his left shin.

'Apologies, Deijan, but you said it was urgent?'

'Barph!' said Sarfelt, licking his knee.

'Can you bring some food for Sarfelt? She's driving me crazy!'

'Affirmative, Deijan. Sentient Alpha Lambda 102 is waiting for your orders.'

The giant face was replaced by a female figure wearing blonde hair and a soft smile.

'Is this the Untold Sacrifice?' said Klesus.

'Affirmative, Deijan. I will be honoured to accept your orders.'

'Hmm, is that so?' said Klesus, fastening his clothes. While he spoke, a tiny vehicle wheeled past him and deposited a pile of slithering worms and insects on the living room floor.

'Not in here!' he cried. 'For pity's sake!'

'I do not understand. Please clarify your orders, Deijan,' said 102. 'Should I terminate this communication?'

'Barph!' said Sarfelt, rushing over to the wriggling mass. She deposited a ball of spit on top of the insects, stretched out her tongue, and tucked in.

'Disgusting animal,' said Klesus, clambering on a reclining chair to escape the heaving mess.

'I am awaiting your orders, Deijan,' said 102, in a tone that sounded almost like mockery.

'Alright, listen up. I want Dr Vex, whatever-his-name-is, to find and protect Aenaid life. He is *not* to destroy or damage anything on Terra Prime without my express permission. Is that understood, 102?'

'Affirmative, Deijan. I will brief Dr Vex at once.'

'Good, I need this mission to be successful and peaceful.'

'Affirmative, Deijan.'

'Alviqua, please confirm my orders.'

'Affirmative, Deijan. Your orders are to find and protect Aenaid life on Terra Prime. In addition, Terra Prime is to remain undamaged.'

'That is correct. I don't want any buildings, cities, continents, or solar systems destroyed. Is that understood?'

'Affirmative,' said 102.

'That is understood, Deijan,' said Alviqua.

'Do I have your word?'

'Please clarify what you mean by *word*, Deijan?' said Alviqua.

'Do you promise?'

'I do not understand your question, Deijan,' said Alviqua. 'Please clarify.'

Klesus groaned.

'I want to know everything that happens on Terra Prime. There must be no surprises.'

'Affirmative, Deijan,' said Alviqua. 'We will report everything.'

'See that you do,' muttered Klesus, making his way to the kitchen.

CHAPTER 3: EXPLORERS

Sean finished his brunch alone. He decided to explore the house while his mother packed her bags and Mrs Campbell washed the dishes. Sean strolled down a long, tiled hallway and passed at least a dozen rooms. He tried a couple of doors and found they were locked. At the far end of the corridor, he reached a familiar-looking entrance hall and one of the highest ceilings he had ever seen. An ornate staircase rose to a landing, where it divided left and right into two sweeping arms. At the foot of the stairs, a pair of marble, Greek warriors stood guard with spears and shields.

Sean noticed a crest at the base of each statue. It was the same design he had seen on the mantelpiece in his bedroom. Beneath the crests, identical words were carved in Greek. He recognised the alphabet from a school project and pieced the words together, letter by letter. In English characters, it read: *Alkter.*

'I wonder what that means?' he mused.

Outside, there was a growl of engines and a crackle of gravel. Doors slammed, and footsteps crossed the driveway. Sean hurried back to the dining room and climbed on a chair to peer out of the window. Two blacked-out vehicles waited on the driveway. Beside them stood a pair of Foundation agents wearing dark suits and sunglasses, which was strange because it was a cloudy day.

'What is it, Sean?' said Mrs Campbell, returning from the kitchen.

'It looks like Mum's lift has arrived.'

There were loud voices in the hallway, and Sean went to see what was happening.

'But Mrs Yeager, we can't protect you in a family car,' said Brawne.

'Fine, but could you make it look any more obvious? I mean - black cars, blacked-out windows, and penguins in dark glasses. Why not put neon signs on the cars as well?'

'I don't follow.'

'But everyone else will be able to, won't they?'

'I promise you these are state-of-the-art vehicles. They carry the latest security equipment, Mrs Yeager.'

'But do they have to be *black*?'

'What colour would you like them to be? Pink?'

Mrs Yeager rolled her eyes.

'Even silver would be less conspicuous.'

'No problem, I'll ask the drivers to have their cars re-sprayed right away,' said Brawne without a hint of humour. 'Now, are you going to visit your aunt or not?'

'Yes, I *am*,' said Mrs Yeager.

Sean caught her eye and allowed himself to be pulled into a hug. Meanwhile, Brawne chatted to the drivers.

'Promise me you'll do everything Mrs Campbell asks and remember to feed the cat.'

'I will,' said Sean, wondering what had become of Tiger.

'I'll only be away for a couple of days; I'll call you every night.'

'*Okay*, Mum,' said Sean, feeling embarrassed in front of Brawne and the assembled agents.

Sean followed his mother and Brawne down the front steps to the waiting vehicles. One of the agents clicked a key fob, and, in a flash, they changed from black to silver.

'Cool!' said Sean.

'Is this colour more to your liking?' said Brawne.

'Well, it's a start,' said Mrs Yeager, handing her bags to an agent.

After the motorcade had departed, a blonde-haired guard in khaki overalls approached Sean. He had a small communicator stuck to his ear, which flashed green every few seconds.

'Hi, Sean, how are you? My name's Hughes. I've been asked to show you around.'

Hughes spoke with an accent Sean was unable to place.

'Agent Hughes?'

'I wish. Hughes is fine. I'm working on the promotion.'

'So, where am I?' said Sean.

'This is Kimbleton Hall. Your presence here is a secret, Sean. And we need to keep it that way. You must *not* disclose your whereabouts to any friends or family. That includes phone calls, text messages, and anything you say on the internet.'

'How come? Isn't this place protected?'

Hughes eyed Sean with a worried expression.

'Hasn't anyone told you what we're up against?'

Sean gave a shrug.

'You know the device you used to break into Krankhausen's base?'

'Err, yeah,' said Sean, wondering how Hughes knew so much.

'Well, Krankhausen's still out there somewhere, and we think he's stolen an arsenal of them.'

Sean remembered Skyraptor-two falling into the sea and swallowed hard.

'So yes, Kimbleton Hall *is* protected, but not against our own weapons. We're on twenty-four-hour alert in case Krankhausen and his mates turn up.'

Hughes led Sean on a tour of the house. It was a large mansion constructed from pale yellow stone and had clusters of chimney stacks rising from its roof. He told Sean how Kimbleton Hall used to be a hunting lodge. It stood on the site of an ancient monastery and the remains of a Bronze Age settlement. They passed a chapel, outbuildings, and a guardhouse. On the eastern side was a walled garden, which Sean was welcome to explore. At the rear of the house, a stone terrace led to an expanse of lawn and avenues of trees.

'Beyond the trees is the perimeter fence and beyond that is the woods,' said Hughes.

'Can we go there?' said Sean.

'No, Sean. It's too dangerous,' said Hughes. 'We can only protect you inside these grounds.'

Sean groaned. The house looked dull compared to the woods, and already he was missing his friends. Hughes looked him in the eye.

'Anything could happen to you out there, Sean. That woods is full of wildlife.'

'Is that why are all the doors downstairs are locked?'

Hughes laughed.

'To keep out wildlife? No, we have a security barrier to do that. But you do need to stay away from the West Wing - it's a restricted area.'

'Why? What's in there?'

'My, you are a nosey parker, aren't you?' said Hughes. 'I could tell you, but then I'd have to turn your brain into soup.'

'Yuck!'

A golden-yellow dog appeared and sprinted across the lawn. It barked and ran towards a cat, which lay sleeping on a step at the far end of the house. All of a sudden, the dog yelped and scampered away, howling. Mrs Campbell appeared and gave chase, shouting as she ran.

'Braveheart! Braveheart!'

The cat skulked around a corner.

'Is that Tiger?' said Sean.

'Sorry, I meant to tell you. It was delivered earlier this morning,' said Hughes. 'It's a strange animal.'

Sean scowled.

'It might seem strange to you, but it's *my* cat.'

Sean strode at pace towards the house pursued by Hughes. Before he could reach the terrace, a fire alarm sounded in the main building. It was joined by a chorus of other alarms that echoed through the building.

'Wait here, Sean. I need to go and see what's happening.'

Sean sat on a low wall and studied the house. There were three floors and at least twenty windows on each. Grey smoke poured from a ground floor air vent in the East Wing, and two fire doors slammed open at the opposite end of the house. A line of figures wearing laboratory coats hurried from the building.

'I wonder what they're doing in there?'

Sean skipped down the terrace steps and crept towards the West Wing concealed by a row of rose bushes.

****

Brigadier Cuthbertson spent his morning reading reports about the St Jacobs incident. He scanned a series of documents looking for mentions of anyone called Yeager. However, there were none.

'Strange,' he thought. 'Perhaps my memory is playing tricks on me?'

'Can I help?' said a familiar voice from the doorway.

Cuthbertson looked up in astonishment.

'Founder? How can I help you?'

Cuthbertson closed his laptop and tried to make his actions look casual. He failed.

'Still looking for information about Sean Yeager?'

'Well, I, err…'

The Founder, Cassius Olandis, was tall and thin with grey eyes and silver-grey hair. He wore a light beige trench coat and was flanked by two shimmering figures.

'There's still the matter of Krankhausen to tidy up,' said Cuthbertson.

'So you thought you would search our restricted files?'

'No, well, I err… Yes, Founder,' said Cuthbertson, feeling brave.

'You can call me Cassius, Henry. What is it you would like to know?'

'I thought Sean Yeager's father was involved in the St Jacobs incident?'

'Yes, he was, but he wasn't called Yeager.'

'Really? So, what was his name?'

Cuthbertson stared into Olandis' eyes which glowed silver and gold.

'It is not important, Henry. Open your mind, and everything will become clear to you.'

Cuthbertson could not tear his eyes away and began to feel very relaxed.

'You will re-instate Captain Ayres. Order him to train a squad of commando cadets in Kimbleton Woods.'

'Yes, Cassius.'

'You will protect Sean Yeager and his family. They are friends of the Foundation.'

'Yes, Cassius.'

'You will order Professor Quark's team to continue their search for Egbert Von Krankhausen.'

'Yes, Cassius. I will.'

In a flash, Olandis whisked a white bottle of pills from Cuthbertson's desk and tucked them in his pocket.

'And you will stop taking pills. I need you to focus on building a submarine. Awake!'

Cuthbertson woke from his trance and looked around in confusion.

'I believe you have some plans for me?'

'Indeed, Henry. We'll need sub-contractors and a shipyard.'

'Of course,' said Cuthbertson. 'But do we have enough money?'

'Send me their quotes, and I'll provide double their estimates. These things always go over budget.'

'May I ask, why is this project so important, Founder?'

'I believe you just have, Henry. Let me know when you have the quotes. Good day.'

In a thrice, Olandis and his bodyguards were gone. Cuthbertson was left staring at a pile of blueprints and data sticks on his desk.

'Submarine, eh?' he announced to an empty office.

He stretched out his arms and rubbed his shoulder. It felt as good as new.

****

Sean waited until all the white coats had assembled on the

rear lawn. He crept along the rear of Kimbleton Hall and ducked below a line of windows. Fire alarms still echoed inside the building, but the smoke had stopped. He reached a fire escape and peered inside. There was a short corridor leading to a room with spotlights in its ceiling. Sean took a few steps inside and noticed a red light twinkle on the wall facing him.

'Hey! Where do you think you're going?' said a voice behind him.

It was Hughes.

'I thought I told you the West Wing is out of bounds?'

Sean put on his most innocent smile.

'Oh, *this* is the West Wing? I thought it was at the other end of the house?'

'Very funny. I can see you're a magnet for trouble.'

'I don't know what you mean.'

'I bet you don't. Mrs Campbell's been looking all over for you,' said Hughes. 'If I take you inside, will you promise to keep out of here in future?'

'I promise,' said Sean, shaking hands to seal the bargain.

Hughes marched through the fire exit.

'Come on then! We don't have all day.'

They entered a wide room with shuttered windows. Suspended from the ceiling were two crystal chandeliers and a metal frame supporting an array of spotlights. At the centre of the room was a circular plate embedded in the floor. Behind it stood a laboratory shaped by thick glass walls and packed with equipment. Around them, computer screens blinked in silence, waiting for their masters to return.

'This used to be the ballroom,' said Hughes, leading Sean to a door on the opposite side.

'What does all this stuff do?'

'Let's leave that to the boffins, shall we?'

Hughes opened a security door and led the way along a wood-panelled corridor and up a flight of steps. They arrived in the library, and a door grated shut behind them. Sean span around, but all he could see was a wall of books and a ladder on wheels.

'How do we get back to the corridor?'

'*You* don't. If I catch you in there again, I'll give you a free holiday in our cells. Understood?'

'Err, yes.'

Hughes took Sean back to the dining room. As they approached, a pungent smell of burned food filled the air. Mrs Campbell appeared, wearing yellow rubber gloves.

'Ah, there you are, Sean. Could you lend me a hand, my love? We've had a little accident.'

'See you later,' said Hughes. 'Remember what I said.'

Sean followed Mrs Campbell into the kitchen and had to stop himself from laughing. There was a dark stain on the ceiling, and the stove was covered in a layer of sticky tar. A blackened pan lay immersed in the kitchen sink.

'Lunch will be late today. Could you hold this chair steady for me?'

Sean helped Mrs Campbell to clean up the kitchen for what seemed like hours. It was tiring work, and they used an array of sprays and scrubbers. By the time they had finished, the kitchen was spotless and smelled of bleach. A clock in the hallway struck the hour, and chimes echoed through the house.

'Time for a sandwich and a cuppa,' said Mrs Campbell.

'Was that your dog running away earlier?'

'Braveheart? He belongs to my daughter, Emily. Something spooked him, that's for sure,' said Mrs Campbell, with a worried look. 'I expect he'll be back when he's hungry. Oh, before I forget, your tutor left a book for you. He said you need to read it before your first lesson.'

'Lesson?' said Sean. 'What lesson?'

****

Greerbo dozed on an uncomfortable mattress in near darkness. He was bored senseless in his cell and had nothing to do. He felt a dry tickle at the back of his throat and coughed. Before long, Greerbo's forehead was covered in tiny beads of sweat. He felt a wave of nausea build up and leaned over a toilet pan. He muttered to himself and waited for his stomach to clear. Instead, unseen by him, three insect-like creatures fell out of his mouth. They bounced on the edge of the stainless steel bowl and dropped onto the floor.

'Yuck!' muttered Greerbo, wiping his mouth on a tissue.

On a screen outside, Quark watched Greerbo. It was not a pretty sight. The prisoner was overweight and looked like a vagrant with buttock cleavage poking out of his trousers.

'Tranquillize the prisoner and bring him to the cryogenics lab in full restraints.'

'Yes, sir,' said Edmondson, the head guard.

He turned to his team, who were dressed in body armour, gas masks, and gloves.

'Gas grenades on my count. Three, two, one, go!'

The first guard opened the cell door, and two others rolled grenades along the floor. Greerbo was taken by surprise. He covered his face and held his breath. Seconds later, three darts pierced his rump, and he let out a cry. It was impossible to resist the sedatives though, and Greerbo crumpled where he stood.

The third guard wheeled in an upright metal trolley, and the team dragged him towards it, feet first. While the guards were busy securing Greerbo to the trolley, three spyder-bots crept, unseen, from the shadows. They extended their pincers and scuttled towards the nearest guard. The first spyder-bot raced around his feet and dug itself into the heel of a boot. However, the guard felt nothing and continued to tether Greerbo's ankles. The second spyder-bot followed suit and attached itself to the guard's other heel. It folded itself up and waited. Meantime, the third spyder-bot moved too slowly and was flattened by Edmondson's weight. He stepped forwards, and the spyder-bot staggered away on damaged legs before collapsing in a corner.

'Right, he's secure. Let's get him to Cryogenics,' said

Edmondson.

The team wheeled Greerbo out into the corridor.

'That was easy,' said a guard. 'I don't know what Greaves' problem was?'

'You know Greaves. He always liked to make a mountain out of a molehill,' said another.

'Don't speak ill of the departed, lads,' said Edmondson.

They approached a corner and slowed to steer the trolley. As they did so, the spyder-bots dropped quietly onto the floor and scuttled away.

'Sorry, sir. Where did Greaves end up?'

'I think they sent him for retraining,' said Edmondson.

'To flip burgers?'

'And learn about personal hygiene?'

'That's enough, lads,' said Edmondson. 'We have a job to do.'

Meanwhile, the spyder-bots cut a tiny hole in the cover of a service duct and climbed inside.

****

A figure wearing blue overalls approached Darius Deveraux's sleeping quarters.

'Master, I have news.'

'What is it, Seventy-one?' said Deveraux, rousing himself from a cot bed.

'Two of our spyder-bots have been activated. They are inside the Foundation's Headquarters.'

'Excellent! Order them to find the communication centre. We need to locate Yeager.'

'Yes, master. It will be done.'

CHAPTER 4: COMMUNICATION

Over tea, Sean asked Mrs Campbell about his tutor. She told him a man called Mr Steele would be arriving in a few days. However, she was unsure what he would be teaching. All Mrs Campbell knew was that Steele had left him some homework.

'But I'm still on holiday!'

'Sorry, Sean. I'm only the messenger. Perhaps they've decided it's not safe for you to return to your old school?'

'But what about my friends?'

Mrs Campbell raised her palms in surrender.

'I'm sure it's for the best, my love.'

'I haven't spoken to anyone for weeks. They'll have forgotten I exist.'

'I don't know what to say,' said Mrs Campbell. 'You can't very well phone them, now can you? Not while this Krankhausen is still at large?'

'I could use OpenLife?'

'Open *what*?'

'It's a website where people chat,' said Sean.

Mrs Campbell gave him a weary look.

'Yes, I know all about those websites, young man. It was all I could do to keep Emily from sharing her every thought with total strangers.'

'But *all* my friends use it.'

'Do they now?' said Mrs Campbell. 'Well, so does a weirdo who asked Emily to marry him.'

Sean gave a half-smile.

'What did she say?'

'She was only nine at the time!'

After nearly an hour of negotiation, Mrs Campbell agreed to allow Sean thirty minutes on the internet. In return, he promised to keep his location a secret. As a precaution, she phoned Brawne, who was far from keen. He lectured her for a considerable time about the dangers of the internet.

However, he finally relented and summoned a technician to prepare Sean's computer. An hour later, Sean was called to the library.

'Everything's ready, your majesty,' said Hughes.

Sean sat in front of a computer screen and did his best to ignore disapproving looks from Hughes and Mrs Campbell.

'You know the rules - no biting, gouging, swearing, or sharing your location on the internet,' said Hughes. 'We have people watching your every keypress. No pressure, Sean.'

'Err, great. Thanks a lot.'

He sat motionless for a few minutes, unable to remember his OpenLife password and afraid of looking a fool in front of his minders. A plan began to form in his mind. It grew legs, a tail, and hatched. Sean mulled it over while pretending to browse a news report. Could it work? It would be much more fun than being stuck in a creepy mansion with boring adults.

Sean typed in his password and trembled with excitement. OpenLife welcomed him, and he noticed Toby Atkins was online. He opened a message box.

'Hi, Toby. How are you?'

'Wow, Sean. Where have you been?'

'Long story. What's happening?'

'Sorry about your house.'

'Why?'

'Didn't you know? They knocked it down.'

'They did what?'

'Demolished it."

'Seriously? When?'

'Last week, I think. Where are you living?'

'With relatives.'

'Are you coming back to school?'

'I don't know.'

'Why? Are you moving away?'

'I don't know yet.'

'Gosh. Perhaps we'll meet in town?'

'I doubt it.'

'Why not?"

'Relatives won't let me.'

'Catch a bus?'

'There aren't any. I need to buy Mum a present, though.'

'Why? Is it her birthday?'

'Yes, next week.'

'They'll have to let you go shopping then?'

'Doubt it. It's like a prison here.'

'Break out?'

'Fat chance.'

'I could meet you in town on Saturday afternoon? Usual place?'

'I wish! Later, dude.'

'Chin up. Later.'

'See you around.'

Sean logged off and leaned back in his chair. He felt angry someone had demolished his house. Or had they? Was it possible Toby had made it up? However, he was a good friend, and it seemed unlikely. Sean remembered all the birthdays and Christmases he had spent at his old house. And now it was just a pile of rubble. His eyes became misty.

'I hate you, Krankhausen!' he whispered.

Footsteps approached, and Sean turned away from the computer.

'Hey, fella. Are you finished?' said Hughes. 'What's up?'

'Did they really demolish my house?'

'Why would they?'

'Because Krankhausen cut a giant hole in my bedroom wall, that's why. I *hate* him!'

'You're not the only one, Sean. We've lost some good people because of that monster. I'll see what I can find out.'

'Thanks,' said Sean.

'I'm not promising anything, mind.'

'And can I…'

'I know what you're going to ask, and the answer is - no way, José.'

'But, I…'

'Need to buy your mum a birthday present in town? Yes, your wicked relatives know all about that,' said Hughes. 'I'm sorry about your house, but there's no way I can take you into town.'

Sean dried his eyes and stared accusingly at Hughes.

'In that case, I want to speak to the Founder.'

Hughes was lost for words. Nobody spoke to the Founder. Not ever. Hughes himself had only met Olandis once, during an inspection. It was said he had an iron will and only appeared when you least expected him. Most Foundation employees were too scared to even mention the Founder in conversation.

'Now,' said Sean.

'That's impossible.'

'Nothing's impossible.'

In a flash, Sean wrenched a mobile phone from Hughes' utility belt and ran for the library door. He skidded across the wooden floor and sprinted as fast as he could.

'Hey!' cried Hughes, coming to his senses.

Sean raced through the dining room and sidestepped the furniture. There was just a chance he could reach the stairs before he was caught.

'Come back here, you little thief!' said Hughes, racing after him.

'What's going on?' said Mrs Campbell, poking her head around the kitchen door.

'He's taken my phone!'

'Who? Sean?'

Sean charged upstairs and tripped on a metal runner. His pursuer was in the hallway seconds from catching him. There was a shout from below.

'Hey! Where do you think you're going?'

Hughes bolted across the entrance hall and planted a foot on a rug. As he pushed off, the rug folded into a crease.

'Woah!' cried Hughes, sliding across the floor.

Sean reached the landing. He ran inside his room and

locked the door. Gasping for breath, he studied the phone. It displayed a key and needed a password or thumbprint to unlock it. Sean tapped in a few numbers without success, and there was a hammering on the door.

'I know you're in there!'

Sean tried a few different combinations.

'Look, I don't blame you for being upset.'

'This is useless,' he muttered.

'If you open the door, I'll ask the powers that be.'

'How can I trust you?'

'Give me back my phone, and you can listen to the call,'

'It must be a valuable phone?' said Sean. 'Does it bounce?'

'Come on, mate. What do you want from me?'

Sean took a deep breath. What *did* he want? He sensed he had the upper hand, if only for a few minutes.

'The truth,' said Sean.

'About what?'

'My house.'

'The truth is, I don't know anything about your house. I'm only a guard, Sean. They don't tell me anything.'

'I don't believe you. How do you know what I did at Krankhausen's base?'

There was silence for a moment, followed by more footsteps.

'You're a legend, mate. The whole Foundation's heard about what you did. It must have taken real guts to land on Krankhausen's platform.'

'And you'll take me shopping tomorrow?'

'I'll do my best.'

'He's telling the truth, Sean. Please open the door,' said Mrs Campbell. 'We're only trying to look after you, dear.'

Sean realised he had reached an impasse. While he did not believe Hughes, he decided to relent. He turned the key and stood back from the door, expecting the worst.

'Thanks, Sean,' said Hughes, looking more relieved than angry.

'It's okay, dear,' said Mrs Campbell. 'We'll help you to find a special present for your mum. Won't we, James?'

'Err, yeah,' said Hughes.

Mrs Campbell gave Hughes an insistent look, and Sean handed the phone back to him.

****

Two spyder-bots examined a bundle of cables inside a dusty maintenance duct. Their eyes glowed on stalks and flashed beams of red light around the vertical shaft. The spyder-bots used clawed feet to haul themselves upwards and scanned for signals as they went. The cabling was attached to a perforated metal track, and whenever a spyder-bot slipped, it stuck a claw around a hole to steady itself.

After a long climb, the spyder-bots twitched and exchanged messages. They extended sharpened feelers and began to cut into cables. One struck a power line and spun around, twitching and sparking. It was about to fall until its companion hurled a silk lasso and caught it around its legs. The stricken spyder-bot swung helplessly above the abyss. Its legs folded, and its eyestalks flickered and faded.

After several seconds of dangling, the spyder-bot rebooted itself and shuddered back to life. It reached out its legs and gripped a cable tie. Apart from a few scorch marks, it was undamaged. Meanwhile, its companion reeled in the silk lasso and transmitted a new message. Together, the spyder-bots followed the power line to a junction and traced it horizontally above a ceiling.

****

'Master, our spyder-bots have found the communications centre,' said Seventy-one.

'Perfect,' said Deveraux. 'Order them to break into the Foundation's network. Sooner or later, they will tell us everything we need to know.'

****

It was almost dark when Sean returned to his bedroom. Mrs Campbell insisted he had a shower, and he did so without a fuss. She reprimanded him for taking Hughes' phone, but she sympathised with Sean about his friends and his home. Mrs Campbell admitted she knew little about the Foundation or Sean's background. As she said herself, she was only the housekeeper. However, her eyes lit up when Sean spoke of his exploits chasing Krankhausen. Mrs Campbell asked if his mother knew, and he begged her to keep the story a secret.

Alone again, Sean switched on his bedside lamp and looked around for his pyjamas. He found them folded under a pillow.

'I suppose it's not so bad,' he thought. 'At least I have a bigger room.'

While he changed, Sean remembered what Mrs Campbell had said about a tutor and a book. He glanced around the room, but there was nothing new or out of place.

'Perhaps he left it downstairs?'

Sean climbed into bed and turned out the lamp. He snuggled under bedclothes, which felt smooth and comforting. Sean closed his eyes and was about to drift off to sleep when an intense light filled the room. Was he dreaming again so soon? Sean wiggled his toes and pinched an ear. No, he was still awake. The brightness shone through his eyelids and made it difficult to sleep.

'What's going on?' he said, sitting up.

There was no reply, and Sean squinted through his fingers. The light came from an object lying on the dressing table.

'At least it's not talking,' he muttered, alighting on the floor.

Sean crossed the room, expecting to find a laptop or tablet computer. To his disappointment, he discovered a shabby old book, which dimmed as he drew near. It had a battered, red leather cover, which was sealed by a beige ribbon. Embossed in its cover were strange symbols that reminded him of Egyptian hieroglyphs. Sean ran his fingertips over the leather and felt it throb. He traced his index finger over a row of angular symbols, and one by one they lit up. Soon, the whole cover was glowing.

'Wow!'

Sean untied the ribbon, and the book fell open. Coloured lights shone from its pages, dazzling his eyes. He stepped back and fell over the sofa at the end of his bed. Sprawled on his back, Sean watched a projection of images dance across the ceiling. At first, they showed a constellation of stars spinning around a giant swirl of gas and dust. A planet sparkled on the far side of a galaxy, and two lights sped across a void into deep space. The projection zoomed in and followed the lights as they raced past a star and approached a blue planet. The craft soared over clouds and oceans before swooping down to a paradise of natural wildlife. They rose, twisting and turning in the sky, before exchanging fire from hi-tech weapons.

The projection showed a tribal leader with elaborately painted skin pointing at the sky. He chanted something and began a slow dance in front of his tribe. Without warning, there were explosions high above, and two balls of fire fell in opposite directions from the heavens. The tribe panicked and ran for cover while fiery debris rained down on their woods home. The sky darkened and settled into a deep, hazy red.

The scene switched to a cave lit by the flicker of an open fire. The same tribal leader wore an elaborate headdress and heavy animal skins. He bowed to a wall of animal paintings and addressed a smaller tribal group. This time, his movements were sombre, and he wailed at each painting in turn. The wall pictures showed a colourful bird fighting a giant snake as they tumbled from the sky. The creatures danced in the air and unleashed a fireball that covered the land in flames. In a later panel, the bird towered over the people and held a staff like a trophy. The tribal leader lay on his stomach in front of this picture and began to chant. He raised and lowered his arms in praise, and the rest of the tribe followed his lead. Without warning, the book slammed shut, leaving the room in near darkness.

'What was *that* all about?' muttered Sean.

He half-expected a reply. Instead, there was silence. Sean went to bed and fell into a deep sleep. That night he dreamt of a light shining deep inside a cave and a murmur of voices.

'Save us! Save us!' they cried.

****

On his way home, Cuthbertson took a phone call in his car. It had been a long day, but he was feeling relaxed and at ease.

'Hello, Cuthbertson speaking.'

'Good evening, sir. Sorry to disturb you.'

'What is it, Brawne? I'm already late for dinner.'

'It's about the Yeager boy, sir. He's asked to go shopping in Yeatsford for a birthday present.'

'Why? Didn't anyone buy him a present?'

'Not for him, sir. It's for his mother.'

'Oh, I see. And why can't he use the internet?'

'Sean says he wants to choose something special in-person.'

'Does he now? And where's his mother now?'

'She's away visiting a relative, sir. Under armed guard.'

Cuthbertson paused for thought as he joined a motorway. For a change, the traffic was moving, and a procession of red lights snaked away into the distance.

'We can't keep him locked up all the time, now can we?'

'Can't we, sir? What about Krankhausen?'

Cuthbertson accelerated into the fast lane.

'He's vanished. We've no idea where he is. The boy can go shopping provided you arrange suitable protection. Have a word with Ayres.'

'Are you sure, sir?'

'Quite sure. He *is* on our side, Brawne. Everyone deserves

a bit of R and R.'

'Yes, sir. I'll make the arrangements,' said Brawne in a resigned voice.

****

Darius Deveraux's submarine rose to periscope depth and waited for an incoming transmission. The tension inside Deveraux's head began to build again, and he felt a familiar presence in his mind.

'Yes, oh great one. We will find the Yeager boy soon.'

After a few minutes, Deveraux recovered his composure and staggered to the control room.

'Seventy-one, where *is* Yeager?'

The creature stared at him with a blank expression and closed its eyes in silent contemplation.

'Master, we intercepted a Foundation message a few seconds ago. Tomorrow morning, Sean Yeager is being taken to a place called Yeatsford, England, to go shopping.'

The two figures shared looks.

'Do we have any forces near Yeatsford?'

'Yes, master. We have sleepers within ten miles of the town.'

Deveraux considered his options. A clue was something, but he needed to capture Yeager.

'Activate our nearest sleepers and androbots. And set a course for England.'

'Yes, master. Where should we go ashore?'

Deveraux studied a map and frowned. It had been a long time since he had planned a land operation.

'Here,' he said, pointing at a stretch of the south coast.

CHAPTER 5: WATCHERS

It was a struggle to keep Skyraptor-one steady in a fierce wind, and Captain Reynard worried they might land in the ocean. Memories of his last mission weighed heavily on his conscience. He was relieved they had lost only three men, but it was still three too many. Never before had Reynard felt such guilt, and it was not a feeling he welcomed. The communications operator gestured in his direction.

'I have a report from the submersible, sir.'

'Go ahead.'

'Manta-four-zero has located the Matteract's homing beacon and is moving in to recover it.'

'Patch me through.'

'Live now, sir.'

'Manta-four-zero, this is Reynard.'

'Go ahead, Captain.'

'When you recover the Matteract, make sure you disconnect its energy cell. We don't want any accidents down there.'

'Affirmative, sir. We'll do our best.'

'Good luck, Manta-four-zero.'

'Thank you, sir.'

Reynard paced the flight deck. Apart from the constant gale, everything seemed quiet. He studied an array of green and orange scopes. There was not a single ship or aircraft for hundreds of miles.

'Have you picked up anything?'

'Not really, sir. Just a phantom reading a few minutes ago.'

'Where?'

'About half a mile above us.'

Reynard shivered. Could Krankhausen still be out there somewhere, watching them?

'What did you pick up?'

'A short burst of high-frequency radiation. It was probably

a glitch.'

'Could it have been a stealth device?'

'Doubtful, it was nothing like a regular energy signature.'

'Or a passing aircraft?'

'No, sir. We'd have seen them on radar.'

Reynard rubbed his weary eyes and tried to sharpen himself up. Was it possible Krankhausen had acquired a new kind of technology?

'Sweep the area on long and short-range scanners. If you spot anything, let me know at once.'

'Yes, sir.'

Reynard wished Manta-four-zero would hurry up and finish its recovery work. He felt helpless playing nursemaid to a submersible and could not wait to return to base.

****

The Untold Sacrifice hovered in a bank of grey clouds and watched Reynard's every move.

'Ship, can we connect to their commander's mind?' said Vex.

'Negative. Directive-372 forbids any mind probes on primitive natives.'

'So I recall,' said Vex. 'And Directive-435 permits any actions necessary to save Aenaid life?'

A light beam appeared in the centre of the bridge. It grew into a giant Aenaid warrior wearing battle-damaged armour.

'Dr Vex, I was present when we approved Directive-435,' said 102 in a gruff male voice. 'Our mission does not require us to surgically alter Terrans.'

'I'm just saying it would speed things up, that's all. I'm not too keen on your new look, by the way.'

'Have you forgotten your mission, Dr Vex?'

'I *know*. I'm just a re-printed clone.'

'Correct. You are here to find Sean Yeager and any Aenaid survivors. That is all.'

'Alright, keep your hair on. Anyhow, I thought 12-59 was

supposed to lead us to this Yeager?'

'Affirmative,' said 102, changing to a female form. '12-59, what information do you have about Sean Yeager?'

A silver, ovoid shape floated towards the centre of the bridge. Three stabilizers emerged from its base, and it settled in an upright position on the deck. Flecks of red and green light flashed around its casing.

'I can confirm the last known location of Sean Yeager,' said 12-59.

'Which is?' said Vex.

'We have reached the precise coordinates.'

'In the middle of an ocean? Yes, I can see him down there now, walking on the water. *Not*!'

'The Terran organization, known as the Foundation, took Sean Yeager somewhere on the vessel we are now scanning,' said 12-59.

'And yet there is no trace of him on this vessel?' said Vex. 'Yeager must be in a dwelling somewhere?'

'Affirmative, the Yeager house is on-screen now,' said the ship.

A large screen flashed into life. It showed a quiet residential street. However, something was missing. In the middle of a row of red brick houses was a large gap enclosed by wood hoarding. The camera zoomed in on a pile of rubble.

'But there's nothing left?' said Vex.

'This is the site of Sean Yeager's house,' said 12-59.

'But it's a wreck! No one's living there. Why didn't you follow Yeager on this Foundation vessel?'

There was no reply. A small red light on the side of 12-59's casing pulsed for a moment, and it sat in silence.

'Err, hello? I asked a question,' said Vex, tapping the spy-bot's outer casing.

102's avatar sped across the bridge between Vex and the spy-bot.

'We recalled 12-59 to report its findings. When it returned, the Foundation had already taken Sean Yeager to a new location.'

'In other words, you lost him?' said Vex, in disbelief.

'That is correct,' said 102

He shook his head.

'And what about this Matteract device they're looking for?'

'The Matteract is a crude anti-matter weapon,' said 102.

Vex whistled a silent tune.

'How did these apes, I mean humans, manage to invent an anti-matter weapon? From what I've seen, they struggle to feed and clothe themselves.'

'That is why you are here - to mix with the Terrans and find out,' said 102. 'What are your orders, Vex Lauricus?'

'You need *me* to figure out this mess?'

'Why else would we bring you back from the dead?'

Vex glared at 102's holographic body.

'Have you sentients ever heard of tact?'

102's avatar stared at him with a confused expression.

'What is *tact*?'

'Precisely,' said Vex. 'I'm already bored of this spying. Take me to the Foundation's Headquarters. And no flashy stuff. We need to remain undetected.'

****

Long rows of fluorescent strip lights bathed an underground warehouse in a harsh, neon glare. It was packed with lines of irregularly shaped objects wrapped in shrunken, plastic sheets. Two dark-suited figures entered and started up a generator, which quickly spread a cloud of steam in the chilled air.

The figures wore navy overalls and nodded to each other as if communicating in a silent language. They connected hoses to a row of plastic bags and opened a series of valves. One by one, the bags inflated to reveal frozen figures dressed in dark grey uniforms. After several hours, the creatures thawed and opened their mouths to breathe.

****

Under the cover of darkness, Darius Deveraux's submarine approached a distant, rocky shore and slowed to a halt. Seventy-one nudged Deveraux, who was asleep in a narrow cot.

'Master, we have reached land. We have activated the androbots, and they await your orders.'

Deveraux opened his eyes and glared.

'Good, tell them to standby for instructions. And order our spyder-bots to damage anything they can find.'

'It will be done. What should our spyder-bots damage, master?'

Deveraux rose and stretched his arms towards the low ceiling. His eyes blazed with intense anger.

'Use your imagination! Order them to cut cables and wires. Order them to light fires! I want the Foundation's Headquarters shutdown.'

'Yes, master. What is imagination?'

Deveraux considered replying, but instead, he let out a deep sigh. He marched to the control room trailed by Seventy-one.

'And what about our sleepers?'

'We have twenty-one sleepers active in the Yeatsford area, master.'

'Excellent! And now we will wait for our prey to arrive.'

'Our prey, master?'

Deveraux grinned.

'Yes, Seventy-one, our prey.'

****

The next morning, Sean finished his porridge in a hurry. He looked forward to meeting his friends in town, but the dreams still lingered at the back of his mind. He reasoned they were caused by the strange book. But who were the voices? And why were they asking him for help?

'Sean? Hello?' said Mrs Campbell, waving. 'Are you awake?'

Startled, Sean looked up. Of course, it was time to get ready.

'I suggest you take a jacket. It's getting chilly now autumn's arrived.'

Mrs Campbell walked Sean to the front door with Braveheart trotting along beside her. The dog sniffed at Sean's trouser pocket and stared at him with two pleading brown eyes.

'Leave him alone, soppy,' said Mrs Campbell. 'Don't mind him, Sean. He's just being greedy.'

The driveway was empty. While they waited, Sean produced a packet of mints and offered one to the dog. Braveheart swallowed it in one go and begged for another.

'Not too many, mind. They're bad for his teeth,' said Mrs Campbell.

The growl of an engine approached from the distance. Moments later, a pale blue supercar arrived at the front gates and revved its engine. It sped down the driveway and hurled stones onto the immaculate lawn like confetti. It reached the fountain, span in an exaggerated circle, and ploughed two long troughs in the driveway. Pieces of gravel pinged on the lower steps and splashed into the fountain. The vehicle pulled up in a cloud of dust, and Brawne stormed out of his office. An agent climbed out of a gull-wing door, and Brawne greeted him with a slow handclap.

'Very *clever*! Who do you think you are? James Bond?'

'Hi, I'm Agent Stafford.'

Stafford's cheeks turned crimson. He smiled and offered Brawne a handshake. However, Brawne ignored the gesture and tapped his earpiece.

'Hughes? Bring a rake to the front steps. Yes, pronto.'

Stafford cast Sean and Mrs Campbell a sideways look and appeared bemused by the reception.

'I hope your skills as a bodyguard are better than your driving?' said Brawne.

'Yes, I err...'

Hughes arrived at a canter and offered Stafford a long-handled rake. Stafford swallowed hard and accepted it with a look of thunder.

'We prefer to keep our gravel *on* the driveway,' said Brawne, stomping back to his office. 'See that you clear up after yourself. And that's an order!'

Stafford froze and cast a dirty look at the rake.

'Nice car,' said Hughes. 'Mind if I drive?'

Stafford laughed.

'You have to be joking?'

'Brigadier's orders. I'm Sean's shadow.'

'Shadow? You look more like a mercenary on tour in the jungle.'

'Nice one, mate. Are we on the same side, or what?'

'Sorry, it's just the err...'

'Reception committee?'

Stafford nodded and stuck out his hand.

'My name's Stafford, Edward Stafford.'

'Jim Hughes,' said the guard, shaking his hand.

Agent Stafford was fair-haired and tall. He wore an immaculate, navy suit and waistcoat, which were now covered in a light film of dust.

'Never mind Brawne,' said Hughes. 'Charm schools weren't invented in his century.'

Stafford gave a wry smile and brushed gravel dust from his suit.

'I'll let you drive if you put on your Sunday best.'

'Why? Are we going to church?'

'No, but we are meant to be Sean's relatives. And you need to lose the jungle gear.'

'Alright, it's a deal.'

Before Hughes could return to his quarters, Mrs Campbell approached and gave the two men a disapproving look through her half-moon glasses.

'When you've quite finished your male bonding session? Can you *please* help Sean to find something special for his mother? It's her birthday.'

Hughes and Stafford glanced at Sean, who was petting Braveheart at the front door, and nodded sheepishly.

Half an hour later, Sean watched the countryside race by from the backseat of Stafford's sports car. Pegasus carried a scent of newness, and its leather seats felt plush and inviting. He sat back and enjoyed the ride.

'Hey Sean, where do you want to go shopping?' said Hughes from the driver's seat.

'Yeatsford.' said Sean.

'Figures, I wasn't planning to go to London. I meant, which shops do you want to go to?' said Hughes.

'Our orders are to keep to the mall,' said Stafford.

'Is that okay, Sean?'

'I guess.'

'How much money did you bring?' said Hughes.

Sean fidgeted in his seat and realised his mistake.

'From your silence, I'm guessing *none,*' said Stafford.

'You've come shopping without any money? After all the fuss you've made?' said Hughes. 'What were you going to do, *steal* a present for your mum?'

'Well, I uh.'

'It's okay, I'll expense it,' said Stafford.

'You have a Foundation credit card?' said Hughes.

'Of course, farm boy,' said Stafford. 'We don't all live in mud huts in the sticks.'

****

Deep within the Foundation's Headquarters, two sets of tiny claws clattered and slid inside a ventilation shaft. They reached a junction and struggled to find grip. The first spyder-bot skated on the tips of its claws and slid towards a vertical shaft. At the last moment, it hurled a line of silk at the roof and teetered over a sheer drop. The second spyder-bot was not so quick to react. It skated on the metal surface, crashed into its colleague, and knocked it over the brink. The silk line gave way, and the two spyder-bots plunged into darkness. They fell, end over end, flashing their lights in all directions.

'Crump! Crump!'

The spyder-bots slammed into the bottom of the ventilation shaft. Stunned by the impact, they lay motionless in a heap, and their light stalks flickered on and off. Eventually, one of the spyder-bots twitched and stretched out a leg. It unpicked itself from its colleague and staggered a short distance, trailing a damaged limb. Using its feelers, it persuaded the second spyder-bot to rise.

After a considerable time, the spyder-bots staggered on into the darkness and plummeted through a metal grille. They landed on polished glass and slid, scratching thin lines into a windscreen until they reached paintwork. They came to a halt on the bonnet of a sleek Foundation vehicle. It was a sports car parked in a garage full of other vehicles. At once, the spyder-bots set to work, cutting every wire and tube they could find.

****

It was a quiet Saturday morning on the outskirts of Yeatsford. A coach pulled into a layby and released a flock of weary people. One of them was a woman laden with shopping. She alighted on the pavement and walked at a slow pace, carrying plastic bags with *Sale* printed on them in large, red letters. She headed for a pedestrian crossing. However, before she arrived, a seizure struck her. Her arms went limp, and the shopping bags fell to her ankles. Her mouth hung open, and she began to stare at the road.

'Are you okay, missus?' said a passing boy.

The woman ignored him and began to rock in a deep trance. The pedestrian crossing changed to green, and she stood frozen, captivated by the traffic. The boy hurried away.

'You're weird,' he muttered.

A huddle of teenagers gathered in a nearby skate park. A few took turns gliding up and down concrete slopes on their bikes and skateboards while the rest stood around chatting. As the day wore on, the skate park drew visitors from all directions. One carried a skateboard and headphones that buzzed with music. He approached the park and waved to his friends. At the top of a grassy mound, he dropped his skateboard and stood silhouetted against the sky. Motionless, he stared at the main road and turned his head slowly from left to right.

'Hey, Sam!' said one of his friends. 'Sam!'

But Sam ignored his cries and shook from head to toe.

'Ignore him. He's only mucking around. He's into zombies and stuff,' said another teenager.

Sam continued to lurch from side to side for close to an hour. He caught sight of a shiny, blue sports car rushing past and started to twitch. His head jerked back, and his eyes became bloodshot.

****

'Master, we have located a pale blue Foundation vehicle heading towards the centre of Yeatsford,' said Seventy-one.

'How do we know it's the Foundation's?' said Deveraux.

'The vehicle's design matches the one in Von Krankhausen's mind probe.'

'The flying vehicle he tried to destroy?' said Deveraux.

'Yes, master. We have calculated there is a ninety-percent chance Sean Yeager is on board.'

'Most enlightening. Activate our androbots. It's time we gave this vehicle an escort. Remember, I want Yeager taken alive. Everyone else is expendable.'

'Yes, master. It will be done.'

CHAPTER 6: PARKING TROUBLE

Hughes joined a four-lane road lined by trees. Vehicles passed on either side, but the traffic was light for a Saturday morning.

'Where to now?'

'Turn right at the end,' said Stafford. 'The mall is just a few blocks away.'

Sean felt a shiver run through his spine.

'Someone's following us.'

'Yeah, about half of Yeatsford,' said Hughes.

'There's nothing on our scope,' said Stafford.

A car exploded on their left and careered into the air. Hughes swerved to avoid it and accelerated away. Stafford spotted three flying shapes in their rearview camera. They were flying above the traffic and fired a volley of energy-bolts.

'Hostiles detected. Take evasive action,' said Pegasus.

'Burn rubber!' said Stafford.

'I'm trying,' said Hughes.

'Hurry, man. They're gaining.'

'Is there any chance of you shooting back?'

'Pegasus, activate manual cannons,' said Stafford, pulling a control pad from the glove box.

Hughes gunned the engine and weaved around slower traffic. Pegasus raced past a speed camera, which flashed for a second before bursting into flames.

'Darn it!' said Stafford.

'You sure roasted that speed camera,' said Hughes.

'Never mind your speeding ticket. Get us to the mall!'

Hughes took a sharp right turn and threw his passengers sideways. An energy-bolt skimmed their roof and incinerated a nearby tree.

'Can't we just fly out of here?' said Sean.

'No,' said Stafford, 'we're not allowed to fly in a built-up area.'

'Even in an emergency?' said Hughes.

'You're not trained. And I could lose my job.'

Sean glanced out of the rear window. He counted six flying craft split into two groups. Their pilots knelt forwards on small black sleds and were difficult to see against the gloomy sky.

'Boom!'

A passing van rolled onto its roof, and Hughes steered around it, screeching all four wheels.

'They're gaining on us!'

A cannon blast from Pegasus hit one of the hostile craft. It swerved into the back of a double-decker bus, and its pilot crashed through an upstairs window. He landed face-down on a seat and lay there dazed for a moment. Meanwhile, the passengers did their best to ignore the dark-suited intruder, as if his sudden arrival was somehow a regular occurrence. A ticket inspector arrived.

'Hey, mate, have you got a ticket?'

The androbot righted itself, ran back down the aisle, and jumped out of the broken window headfirst. It somersaulted in mid-air, landed on a car roof, and sprinted away after its colleagues.

'Young people today…' said an elderly passenger.

Pegasus accelerated around a corner and under a concrete bridge. Two hostiles had almost caught up, but they misjudged their speed. One flew over the bridge and crashed into an office block. The second scraped just under the bridge and struck a row of orange ceiling lights. Its pilot was unseated and fell backwards into the road. Meanwhile, the craft flew on, skewed sideways, and exploded against a wall.

'In there,' said Stafford, pointing at an entrance labelled: *Staff only.*

Hughes smashed through a barrier and headed for a row of glass doors at one end of the mall.

'Where now?' said Hughes.

'Inside!' said Stafford.

Pegasus mounted a curb and skidded to a halt. As it did so, a man wearing a fluorescent bib appeared and gestured to them.

'Hey, you can't park there! This is a staff car park!'

Stafford hauled Sean out of the car.

'I meant *through* the doors.'

'Call me squeamish, but I'm not into head-on collisions,' said Hughes.

The parking attendant blocked Hughes' path and pointed at Pegasus.

'I need you to move this vehicle *at once,* or I'm calling the Police.'

Hughes shoved him aside.

'Go ahead. And while you're at it, tell the Police about *them*!'

A group of androbots had gathered at the entrance to the car park like a gang of bikers. They spread out to block the road.

'Pegasus, auto-protect system on,' said Stafford, ushering Sean and Hughes towards the shopping centre.

'Armed and ready,' said Pegasus.

The parking attendant eyed the hovering androbots and jabbed his finger in their direction, unsure what to do next. Before he could utter another word, the air was filled with energy-bolts and missiles. The exchange was brief and brutal. The androbots fired and missed, shattering the glass entrance to the shopping mall. In return, Pegasus unleashed a volley of heat-seeking missiles and plasma bolts. In the process it destroyed three androbots and numerous cars. Meantime, the remaining androbots scattered and launched an aerial bombardment. Energy-bolts struck Pegasus on its roof and exposed side. It was thrown against the curb and rolled over a row of concrete bollards. Pegasus smashed through a plate-glass window and came to rest lying upside down in the shopping mall. Meanwhile, the parking attendant crawled away on his hands and knees to a chorus of wailing car alarms. The staff car park resembled a war zone.

****

Quark's team was busy inspecting cars in the vehicle pound.

'Professor, they've all been sabotaged,' said a technician.

'Impossible!' said Cuthbertson, brushing Quark aside and marching past a row of cars.

Cuthbertson climbed into his personal sports car and slammed the door. He started up its engine, which gave a brief clunk and died. He tried to get out and discovered the door was locked tight. Enraged, he thumped on the driver's window but no one was in earshot. A short while later, Quark's phone rang.

'Quark here.'

'It's Cuthbertson. I'm stuck in my infernal car!'

'So, it *is* possible?'

'Get me out of here, Quark!'

'I'll be right with you, sir.'

While Cuthbertson waited to be rescued, a voice came through on an emergency channel.

'Control, this is Stafford. We are under attack! Send help immediately! There are androbots everywhere.'

Cuthbertson tried reply, but none of the car's controls would respond. He resorted to using his phone and ordered Captain Ayres to report to the vehicle pound. Meanwhile, Quark summoned a technician.

'We'll have to cut him out,' said the technician, hurrying to the stores.

Ayres arrived accompanied by three burly commandos.

'Reporting as ordered, Professor. Where's the Brigadier?'

'He's on a phone conference,' said Quark. 'Follow me.'

Quark led the commandos to the far end of the car park. He opened a sliding door and switched on some lights to reveal an expansive storage space. On one side, stood a row of machines covered in heavy tarpaulins. Quark unveiled one and stood back.

'We have a team of agents caught up in a fire-fight at Yeatsford shopping centre. I need your men to help them.'

'Sure, no problem,' said Ayres. 'Fleet can fly us over there in a few minutes.'

Quark shook his head.

'I wish we could. However, Skyraptor-one is on a mission, and Skyraptor-two is being repaired. Our Hoverlifters are too visible, and our Hyperjets are on their way back from Redoubt Island.'

'What about the carpool?' said Ayres.

'Immobilized. Every single vehicle has been sabotaged.'

'So, what about this... *bike*, Professor?'

'We discovered them last year in a deep storage facility.'

Ayres and his men crowded around the strange machine. It resembled a cross between a motorbike and a snowmobile, except it had no wheels. A long, swept seat met a triangular cross-section and a fluted skid ran along its underside. A flattened, conical nose and windshield protected the rider, and two exhaust grilles extended from its rear. The vehicle stood upright and was covered by a thin layer of dust.

'What is it?' said Ayres.

'This is a Glidebike,' said Quark.

'How does it work?'

'We looked for a manual in the archives. All we could find was this.'

Quark handed Ayres a frayed sheet of paper. Printed on one side was a single sentence.

'Activate the voice link by gripping the handles and placing your right thumb on the touch plate.'

Ayres eyed the machine with suspicion.

'Do we know what it's capable of?'

'Not really,' said Quark. 'We considered testing one of them several years ago, but it was never a priority. We believe they respond to regular steering, and all the usual verbal instructions.'

Ayres eyed the machine thoughtfully.

'And who's involved in this fire-fight, Professor?'

'Nine agents and one guard. The hostiles seem to be after Sean Yeager.'

'*Again*? What is it with that kid?' said Ayres, shaking his head.

Quark tapped his nose.

'All I can tell you is that Sean Yeager is very important to our mission.'

Ayres took a deep breath and glanced at the faces of his men. They each nodded.

'Alright, we'll do it. Squad, fetch your body armour and weapons on the double.'

'Yes, sir!' said the commandos, hurrying away.

When his squad had departed, Ayres turned to Quark.

'Are these machines going to work, Professor?'

'Of course,' said Quark. 'All they require is a little focus. I'll take you through the basics.'

****

While Hughes covered their retreat, Stafford dragged Sean through a crowd of shoppers. Alarms rang out from the far end of the mall, and security staff brandishing walkie-talkies hurried to investigate. Shoppers milled around like herds of sheep, oblivious to the drama outside.

'In here,' said Stafford, heading for a department store.

'What's your plan?' said Hughes.

'To stay alive long enough to be rescued.'

'What about *them*?' said Sean, indicating the shoppers.

'Best worry about your own skin,' said Hughes. 'Come on.'

The trio entered a ground floor cosmetics department and weaved around a maze of glitzy display cases.

'Doof!'

A shelf of perfume bottles erupted beside them, drenching customers and shop assistants in a noxious cocktail of scent and glass.

'Move!' cried Hughes. 'This whole place stinks.'

Another detonation threw eyeliner and blusher into the air, covering passers-by in black and red pigment. Customers screamed and fled deeper into the store.

'Upstairs,' said Stafford.

Sean and Hughes waded through a sea of terrified shoppers and reached a deserted escalator. It sat motionless, blocked by a chain barrier and a sign that read: *Out of order*. Sean unclipped the chain and scampered up the metal steps trailed by Stafford and Hughes. Another blast struck a display stand and threw shards of crockery in all directions.

'Control, we could use some help over here.'

'Agent Stafford, your backup team is engaged in a fire-fight close to your current location.'

'Tell them to get a move on, will you?'

An energy-bolt struck the escalator a few steps below him and melted a hole the size of a beach ball all the way through to the escalator's shaft. Stafford raced up the last few steps and pulled out his sidearm.

'Hughes, get over here! We need to hold them off for as long as we can. Sean, see if you can find a fire escape.'

A few customers wandered around on the upper floor, uncertain what the fuss was about.

'This one's out of order. Take the stairs,' said Stafford.

A boy noticed the weapon in Hughes' hand.

'I want one of those!'

'Trust me, kid, you really don't,' said Hughes. 'I'd run home if I were you.'

'You can put it on your list for Santa,' said his father, herding the boy towards the stairs.

For a few minutes, there was calm. Sean noticed a sports department nearby. He browsed its shelves and selected a baseball bat, a skateboard, and a tube of tennis balls. A sales assistant watched him rip open their packaging.

'And how are you going to pay for those, young man?'

'He'll pay,' said Sean, pointing at Stafford.

The assistant noticed Stafford's weapon and hurried away

to find a superior.

Meanwhile, a dark grey figure appeared at the bottom of the escalator. It crouched and fired, melting part of the handrail. Stafford returned fire and struck the androbot's chest. It staggered back twitching, and a weapon fell from its grasp.

'I need you to lie face down on the floor and spread out your arms!' cried a voice below.

It was a police officer armed with a Taser.

'Don't do it, officer! Run for your life!' cried Stafford.

The androbot raised an empty hand towards the policeman, who seemed puzzled by the gesture.

'This is your final warning. Lie face down on the floor, or I'll fire!'

A bolt of blue energy surged from the androbot's wrist and struck the police officer in his midriff. As he fell, he unleashed the Taser. Its wires spiralled through the air and struck a mannequin dressed in a ladies' outfit. The mannequin's body sparked, and smoke issued from its head. Meanwhile, the androbot recovered its weapon and limped out of sight.

****

Darius Deveraux watched a live video stream of the battle from his control room. An infrared camera followed three figures in a deserted department store, and he grinned at what he saw.

'Order the androbots to take Yeager alive. Eliminate the other two. They are of no consequence.'

'Yes, master. It will be done,' said Seventy-one.

****

Without warning, the department store's lights went out. Hughes peered into the gloom.

'I can hear them coming.'

'You're not wrong,' said Stafford. 'Control, where's our nearest exit point?'

'Two hundred yards from your current location. Your phone app will guide you.'

Emergency lights came on, and Stafford spotted Sean crouched between two aisles, his arms full of sports equipment. Stafford crept nearer, and a volley of energy-bolts struck the ceiling above him.

'Get to the fire exit, Sean!'

However, two dark figures blocked Sean's route to a glowing, green exit sign. He hurled a tennis ball at one, and in an instant it fired. The ball exploded in a cloud of yellow fluff. Sean ducked and ran to the far end of an aisle, while toys exploded on the shelves around him.

'Stay down!' cried Stafford, as another dark figure closed in.

Sean mounted the skateboard, pushed frantically on the floor, and readied the baseball bat. He had almost skated past an androbot's grasp when it stuck out a leg and sent him sprawling. A blast wave struck the creature, and it was hurled sideways, flattening a rack of sports shoes.

'Go, Sean! Run!' cried Stafford.

Sean reached the fire escape. He smashed a glass cylinder and forced open a pair of heavy doors. A piercing alarm sounded, and he ran out into daylight. He reached an empty stairwell and hurried down the first flight of steps. Seconds later, an androbot smashed through a landing window and dived onto a lower level. It brushed broken glass from its overalls and peered up at him through a narrow reflective visor.

'Get away from me, you freak!' cried Sean, brandishing the baseball bat.

The androbot raised a hand and exposed a row of tubes in its wrist. It fired a volley of darts, but Sean dodged to one side, and they pinged harmlessly against the concrete steps. The androbot shook its head and extended a fingertip to reveal a sharp needle. It beckoned to him, and Sean panicked.

'Watch, alive. Help me!'

The androbot flexed its thighs like a grasshopper and leaped up the stairs in a single bound. Sean swung his bat at the creature's chest, but the androbot wrenched it from his grasp and dropped it casually into the stairwell. Terrified, Sean ran back to the fire escape. More detonations sounded in the toy department, but there was no sign of Stafford or Hughes. The androbot lunged forwards and grabbed hold of Sean's wrist. It raised its needle finger and prepared to stab him.

'Watch, protect me!' cried Sean.

An aperture opened in his watch and a piercing beam of red light struck the androbot's visor. It cradled its head in its hands and let out a scream.

'Get away from that thing, Sean!' said the watch. 'This is Captain Ayres. Meet me at street level.'

Sean raced down the stairs as fast as his legs would carry him. Behind him, a blaster bolt rang out, and the androbot plummeted past him in the stairwell.

'Hurry, Sean!' cried Stafford, emerging from the shop.

'Where's Hughes?'

'Doing his job.'

At the bottom of the stairs, Sean crashed through another fire escape and paused outside. Moments later, he was joined by Stafford.

'Exit Point, one hundred feet ahead,' said Stafford's phone.

'This way!'

Two androbot craft appeared at tree height and swooped down to attack. They fired a broadside of energy-bolts and devastated a row of shop fronts. Sean cowered behind a concrete waste bin and waited, trembling.

'Sean! This way!'

Stafford had reached a green, portable toilet parked a short distance away in the middle of an open square. He waved to Sean.

'Over here! Run!'

'To a toilet?'

Before Sean could move, an androbot rammed its sled into a shop window between him and Stafford. It staggered from the wreckage and raised its weapon. Stafford aimed his blaster and tried to fire, but nothing happened. In frustration, he ran and threw his weapon at the creature. The androbot shrugged off his attack and fired at Stafford, forcing him to dive and roll.

'Go around it, Sean! You can do it!'

Sean watched the androbot with wary eyes. It aimed an arm and fired. He ducked, but he moved too late. One dart skimmed his left arm, and another struck his right. Sean staggered and fell to the pavement. Meantime, Stafford lunged at the androbot unarmed. However, before he could make contact, an energy-bolt struck the creature's back, and it collapsed where it stood.

Stafford came to lying in a puddle of white liquid. A gloved hand reached down and hauled him to his feet. It was Captain Ayres.

'Come on, Staffy. We need to get Sean to a medic.'

'Better late than never.'

'Blame the traffic,' said Ayres.'

Together, they carried Sean to the green portable convenience and opened its door. Inside, was an empty space reinforced by armour plate, with a chute in the roof and a sprung floor.

'I'll never get used to these things,' said Stafford.

'Pleasant trip,' said Ayres, closing the door.

Stafford reached up to a switch above the door and slid it to one side. He pressed his thumb on a blue pad.

'Collection port active,' said a male voice. 'Awaiting rescue craft. Standby, rescue in two minutes.'

An interior light flashed, and a few moments later, a blast of air threw them skyward. Stafford woke on the deck of a Skylifter with Sean lying beside him, barely breathing.

'Medic!' cried Stafford, raising an arm.

'What have you done to him?' said a figure, kneeling

beside him.

'Kept him alive, mostly,' said Stafford, rolling on his side and wincing. 'There's a dart in his arm.'

'Got it. Relax, we'll be at Kimbleton Hall in a few minutes.'

The medic gave Sean an injection and waved smelling salts under his nose. He let out a groan.

'Sean? Can you hear me? Sean?'

CHAPTER 7: NEWS REPORT

Dr Hassan prised open an ornate wooden casket painted blue and gold. Inside, he discovered an object the size of his fist wrapped in a rough, woven fabric. He opened the tattered cloth and revealed a piece of metal shaped like an oval pebble. Hassan traced a finger over its upper surface and felt his nail catch against a row of tiny indentations.

'An inscription,' he muttered.

He placed the object back into the casket and looked around for a torch. A sound of footsteps echoed from the shadows.

'Who's there?'

'Dr Hassan, I presume?'

In the entrance to the chamber stood a tall figure wearing a beige trench coat and a wide-brimmed hat.

'Who are you? How did you get past the guards?'

'I'm from the International Foundation for Antiquities.'

'I don't understand,' said Hassan.

'My name is Professor Aden,' said the silver-haired man, offering his hand. 'I'm told you've found something of interest?'

'Yes, it's incredible; a tablet from the Eighteenth Dynasty. But how do you find out about it?'

'News travels at the speed of light these days,' said Aden. 'Shall we?'

The two men stooped to inspect the casket, which lay in an empty burial chamber.

'The inscription on the lid suggests it dates from the reign of Akhenaten,' said Hassan, pointing at a row of Egyptian hieroglyphs.

'If not earlier,' said Aden.

Hassan held the tablet under his torch.

'This tablet is made from a heavy alloy. And look, it has symbols cut into it!'

'Do you recognise the language?' said Aden.

'It's unlike anything I've ever seen,' said Hassan, shaking his head. 'It's not Egyptian. Nor any kind of cuneiform writing I can recognise.'

'And what about the murals?' said Aden, gesturing to paintings on the chamber walls.

Hassan took a deep breath and waved his torch at different sections of the hieroglyphs.

'It seems Pharaoh instructed his officials to protect this cavern from all living souls for eternity.'

'He always was a worrier,' said Aden. 'And with good reason as it turned out.'

Hassan looked at him in surprise.

'May I?' said Aden, reaching towards the tablet.

Hassan frowned, reluctant to share his discovery.

'I've never heard of this *Foundation* of yours. Who are you?'

Aden's eyes shone silver. A golden flame grew in the centre of his pupils and spread across both irises. Hassan offered the tablet with a trembling hand. As he did so, the inscription began to glow.

'Thank you for looking after this, Dr Hassan,' said Aden, taking the tablet.

'But you can't take it! This tablet is unique. It's a missing link in our history.'

Aden nodded.

'Indeed it is. Now, if you'll excuse me?'

'Where are you going?' said Hassan, his face flushed.

'Open your mind, and everything will become clear to you.'

When their eyes met for a second time, Hassan's body trembled, and his lenses reflected a golden fire. He shuffled away in a trance and collected his torch. Aden slipped the tablet inside his coat pocket and tipped his hat. He turned to leave the chamber.

'It's a shame about the tomb robbers, Dr Hassan. A terrible shame.'

****

The Untold Sacrifice raced through the Earth's atmosphere, shielded from detection by force fields. It hovered, unseen, two miles above a park containing a vast white building.

'Dr Vex, we have arrived at the Foundation's Headquarters,' said 102, assuming the appearance of a fleet officer.

Vex examined the scene below and sneered.

'Is that the best the Terrans can do? We could erase their building in seconds.'

102's hologram grew three feet taller and changed into a fleet admiral.

'If our mission was to destroy the Terrans, we would not need *you*,' she said, projecting a terse sneer.

Vex scowled. How could he complete his mission and escape the clutches of this annoying sentient? Or perhaps they had already placed an implant inside his brain?

'Yes, Dr Vex, we have,' said 102. 'It was considered essential for the success of this mission.'

'Then I insist you take it out! It's contrary to a dozen Aenaid directives to spy on your own kind.'

102's image shimmered for a few seconds.

'I have reviewed all our directives, and you are correct, Dr Vex. It *is* considered unethical to monitor Aenaid kind in this way.'

Vex clenched his fist in triumph.

'However, you are a clone reproduction of a deceased Aenaid warrior,' said 102. 'Which means you are not a *true* Aenaid life-form.'

Vex let out a stream of curses and waved his arms in rage.

'Dr Vex, you will cease in thirty seconds unless you calm yourself,' said 102 in a deep male voice.

'Cease?' said Vex, shocked.

'Affirmative, we can grow another clone to replace you whenever we choose.'

Vex shook from head to toe. He took several deep breaths and tried to regain his composure. There had to be a way out of his predicament, but how?

'You are correct, Dr Vex. You have two options: co-operate or cease to exist,' said 102.

'Then why don't you use one of your bio-bots instead of me?'

'They are here to assist you, Dr Vex. We need your operational experience. What are your orders?'

Vex stood upright and recalled his military training from many years ago. He was seething but did his best to control his emotions.

'I need the current location of this Sean Yeager. Instruct 12-59 to scour the Foundation's sources and find out where he is.'

'Affirmative.'

Vex watched 12-59 hover out of the bridge. The ship's avatar flickered and vanished in a flash of light. Vex flinched and shielded his eyes.

'And I need to retain my sight!' he said, as a bright orange spot glowed inside his eyes.

****

Brigadier Cuthbertson questioned Professor Quark like an over-enthusiastic parent.

'And where were our agents when the ambush occurred?'

Quark adjusted his glasses and prepared to answer for the fifth time.

'Our agents surrounded Yeatsford shopping centre, Brigadier. However, they were outnumbered by hostile forces.'

'And what have we told the Police?'

'Our public-relations people reported some information about a terrorist threat from extremists.'

'Which we made up?'

'Not exactly. We gave them some unconnected facts and

allowed them to draw their own conclusions.'

Cuthbertson frowned.

'So we lied?'

'Not as *such*,' said Quark, screwing up his face to suggest Cuthbertson was, in fact, correct.

'Does the Founder know?'

Quark looked puzzled.

'I don't know. No one's seen him for days.'

'And who's in charge of the clean-up operation?'

'Captain Ayres, assisted by my bio-research team.'

Cuthbertson smiled.

'Excellent, I see everything is under control. Now, if you'll excuse me?'

'I beg your pardon?' said Quark. 'Our security is like a sieve. Our vehicles are write-offs, and we've only just survived an ambush by ruthless androbots.'

'Precisely. But we have *survived*. Now all we need to do is tidy up the mess. I have every confidence in you, Professor,' said Cuthbertson, resting a hand on Quark's shoulder.

Quark was lost for words.

'Who is this man?' he thought. 'Do I know him?'

'If you need anything, give me a call,' said Cuthbertson, returning to his reading.

'Fine,' muttered Quark out of earshot. 'If that's how it's going to be.'

Quark returned to his office and set to work. He reasoned that since Cuthbertson had given him free rein, he would make the most of the opportunity. Quark decided to use all the people and technology at his disposal.

'Captain Ayres? Quark here; I need you to arrange some cold storage vans to bag up the hostiles and ship them to our labs. The Police? Oh, tell them there's a risk of infection. Thank you.'

Next, he contacted his lead technician.

'Fullbright? Quark here. We have a code red alert. Release our prowler-bots and activate the new security system. What do you mean, when? Now! Thank you.'

And last but not least, the Medical Department.

'Dr Fettale? Yes, it's Professor Quark. How is our patient? You've removed the dart? Excellent. Are there any signs of permanent damage? Good. Yes, he can return to Kimbleton Hall. Ask Captain Reynard to make the arrangements.'

Quark gave a contented sigh. It felt good to be in charge.

****

Darius Deveraux hissed in frustration. He stabbed a finger into a three-dimensional image of Yeatsford Shopping Centre and distorted the outer wall of the mall.

'*How* did they rescue Yeager? We had them surrounded!'

Seventy-one closed its eyes. The projection changed to show a group of coloured shapes hovering outside.

'Foundation reinforcements arrived and outflanked our forces,' said the androbot, in a steady voice.

'But how? We disabled all their vehicles!' said Deveraux.

'That is incorrect, master. The reinforcements arrived on…'

Deveraux slammed his fist on the table and glared at his second-in-command. He shuddered at the thought of another encounter with Vrass.

'And where is Yeager now?'

'On his way to a Foundation site called Kimbleton Hall,' said Seventy-one.

'Hmm,' said Deveraux. 'This time, we must leave nothing to chance. Feed the Constructor. We have need of its abilities.'

'Yes, master,' said Seventy-one, hurrying to the far end of the submarine.

****

Dr Vex's meal was interrupted by a holographic flash of light in the galley. He groaned and shielded his eyes.

'You nearly gave me a heart attack! Can you please stop

doing that?'

'I have urgent news,' said 102.

'And I only have *one* heart. What is it?'

'12-59 has reported a battle involving Foundation forces and Sean Yeager.'

'A battle? Who are they fighting?'

'We have insufficient information to answer your question.'

Vex disposed of his meal tray in the recycling machine. It hummed in response.

'Get me down there. I need to know what's going on.'

'You are too late, Dr Vex. The battle is over. Sean Yeager has been removed from the area.'

'And do you know where he is?'

'Affirmative, we are tracking his journey to a place the Terrans call Kimbleton Hall.'

Vex grinned. He pictured blue skies and clouds to conceal his true thoughts.

'Keep tracking Yeager. I'm going down to investigate this battle.'

102 flickered for a few seconds before replying.

'Affirmative, our probes will follow Sean Yeager. However, your mission does not require an investigation of this Terran conflict.'

Vex scowled and replied in a measured voice.

'To find and secure this Yeager, I need to know who is threatening him because that threat is likely to return.'

102's avatar vanished while it considered his request. It returned in the form of a female fleet officer, wearing a serene, otherworldly expression.

'Dr Vex, your reasoning is sound. We will prepare the ship for a landing on Terra Prime.'

'Mind you don't land on anyone.'

'We have procedures for landing and concealment, Dr Vex,' said 102 in a dismissive tone. 'This ship will not land on any life forms.'

****

Two commandos carried Sean by stretcher to his bedroom. Sean felt drowsy, and his arm throbbed inside its bandage.

'Chin up, lad. You'll soon be right as rain,' said one of the commandos as they lowered him onto his bed.

Mrs Campbell appeared, carrying a tray and a bowl of chicken soup.

'Goodness, what happened? Are you okay, my love?' she said, setting the tray on his bedside table.

A phone rang, and Mrs Campbell retrieved it from an apron pocket.

'Hello? Mrs Yeager? How are you? I'm glad to hear it. Sean? Yes, he's been as good as gold. He's right here with me. Would you like a word?' she said, raising her eyebrows.

Sean frowned and accepted the handset.

'Hi, Mum,' he said, with as much enthusiasm as he could muster. 'I'm a bit tired. Yes, I'm in my room. Sorry, I forgot to feed the cat. Yes, I'll feed him before bedtime. Everything's fine. Bye. Bye.'

Sean handed back the phone and let out a sigh. Mrs Campbell gave a wise nod.

'What happened? They wouldn't tell me a thing.'

After a lengthy discussion about not distressing his mother, Mrs Campbell swore herself to secrecy. Sean told the story of his shopping trip.

'It was all over the news,' said Mrs Campbell. 'They said it was a protest by students outside the Luke Harris department store.'

'Did they mention flying craft and blasters?' said Sean.

Mrs Campbell shook her head.

'No. Why?'

'The attackers were dressed in black overalls and fired darts out of their wrists,' said Sean.

'And they knocked you out?' said Mrs Campbell.

'Yes, one of them shot me in the arm.'

'Poor thing. Finish your soup, and we'll see about your cat. I tried to feed it earlier, but it didn't seem very interested.'

Sean sat up in bed and gulped down the soup before devouring two slices of bread and butter.

'Would you like some more, dear?'

Sean nodded.

'Have you seen Hughes anywhere?' he said between mouthfuls.

****

Inside a cordon of blue tape, detectives surveyed a damaged shopping mall and mingled with soldiers. Vex moved unseen between groups of huddled figures and listened to their conversations. A soldier wearing a facemask stood beside a body bag and argued with a plainclothes police officer.

'And my orders are to take them to the pathology lab,' said the detective.

'But there's a serious risk of infection. This is a matter for Military Intelligence,' said the soldier.

'Look, you can't remove evidence from a crime scene!'

'It's a diseased and very dead terrorist. Take a look if you don't believe me,' said the soldier, pulling on latex gloves and unzipping the body bag.

A stream of white liquid oozed out of the bag, and the detective took a step back. He reached for his phone.

'I'll have a word with my superiors.'

Vex kept to the shadows and was careful not to bump into anyone. Outside the shopping mall, a truck strained to lift a large green box, labelled *Klean Flush*, with an extended crane. Its motor revved, and the crane's arm reached across the square, almost tipping over the truck.

At the far end of the cordoned area, a body bag lay undisturbed. It rustled and wriggled on the concrete without anyone noticing. Vex kept to a safe distance and watched a cut appear in the bag. A distorted hand emerged and tore the plastic open. Vex watched a blade vanish inside one of its fingertips and took refuge behind a concrete pillar. Even in his camouflaged battlesuit, he felt helpless without a weapon.

In one continuous movement, a dark grey figure rolled out of the body bag. As it turned over, it changed into a Terran adult wearing trousers and a check shirt. The figure stood beside an ornamental tree, its face obscured by a baseball cap.

'Hey, what are you doing?' said a uniformed police officer. 'You're not allowed in here!'

The figure said nothing and allowed itself to be escorted away. Vex watched it stride confidently between a row of parked vehicles. It ducked under a line of blue tape and hurried into a crowd. Vex tailed the figure at a safe distance and watched it enter a nearby office building. He was about to follow when a voice filled his mind.

'Dr Vex, return to the ship immediately. You have a mission to complete.'

CHAPTER 8: LEGEND

Evening sunlight covered Sean's bedspread in a golden glow. He reflected on his androbot encounter and prayed that Hughes had somehow escaped. Drifting in and out of sleep, Sean felt the brush of a furry tail tickle his cheek.

'Tiger?'

He rolled over and opened his eyes. Sure enough, a cat with vertical ginger stripes on its face sat on the pillow beside him. It stared accusingly at him through a pair of bright, sapphire eyes.

'Tiger? Where have you been?' said Sean, sitting upright. 'And why aren't you eating?'

The cat tipped its head a few degrees to one side and spoke without moving its lips.

'Have you tried eating the muck they call cat food?' it said, in a clear, male voice.

'Tiger?' said Sean.

'And they told me you were bright?' said the cat.

'You're not my cat!' said Sean, moving towards the edge of the bed. 'Where's Tiger?'

'Ten out of ten for observation,' said the cat, feigning a smile.

'What have you done to him?'

'I haven't done anything to *her,* Sean. For all we know, your beloved Tiger is still wandering around somewhere, purring at random strangers for food.'

'Then what are you, a robot?'

'Faster than a speeding bullet,' said the cat, stretching its back into an arch.

'Who sent you?'

'The Foundation, of course. I'm here to protect you.'

Sean slid out of bed and kept the cat at a safe distance.

'How are *you* going to protect me?'

The cat looked insulted and raised a paw to reveal a row of

sharp claws.

'I have my methods.'

'You're going to use claws against laser blasters?' said Sean.

'Actually, androbots are equipped with plasma cannons and poison darts,' said the cat. 'You may have noticed?'

'And where were *you* when I was attacked?'

'Patrolling.'

'Patrolling where?'

'This house has a lot of nooks and crannies. It's my job to search them for intruders.'

Sean studied the cat. It had similar proportions to Tiger and the same ginger and white coloured fur. However, it looked heavier and more menacing.

'Show me.'

'No way. It would be far too dangerous in your condition.'

'Then how can I trust you?' said Sean.

'I'm your pet,' said the cat, curling its tail around its body and making a purring sound. 'Don't you just *love* me?'

Sean backed away.

'You're not very clever for a robot, are you?'

'Touché!' said the cat. 'I think you'll find I'm more intelligent than you are.'

Sean gave an ironic snigger and switched on a bedside lamp. He winced at the discomfort in his arm.

'Oh really? I bet you can't tell me anything I don't already know.'

'Try me.'

'Why did Krankhausen steal all my things?'

'Because he wanted your DNA.'

'What's DNA?'

'Don't they teach you anything at school?' said the cat, raising its eyes towards the ceiling. 'Your genetic make-up. The chemical design of who and what you are. Your cellular blueprint.'

Sean nodded.

'And why does he need my DNA?'

'To clone you, of course.'

Sean raised his eyebrows.

'Why me?

'We're not sure.'

'If that's all he wanted, why did Krankhausen knock down my house?'

The cat paced his bed.

'He didn't. The council did. They declared it unfit to live in,' said the cat. 'Don't you want to know about your father?'

Sean took a sharp breath. Was it possible this cranky, feline robot knew about his father?

'Where is he?' said Sean.

'We're not sure. He was lost after a mission on the island of St Jacobs. The Foundation tried to rescue him, but we found no trace.'

'What was he doing there?'

'Working for the Foundation. He helped to save thousands of lives.'

Sean yawned and rubbed his eyes.

'You need to rest. We can talk again tomorrow.'

The cat stood up, strolled across the bed, and jumped on the floor.

'I'll be outside if you need me,' it said, leaping up to a windowsill and scrambling through an open skylight.

While he slept, Sean pictured flying craft and androbots. He imagined Hughes surrounded and fighting for his life. He attempted to reach him, but every fire door he pushed was either locked or guarded by an androbot. Later, the murmuring voices returned. A chorus of voices repeated the same words over and over.

'Save us. Save us.'

****

Major Clavity waited impatiently for his appointment. He paced an empty office and tried a variety of seats. For a time, he watched exotic fish display their finely plumed fins as they glided around a tropical tank. They shimmied and danced in the water, reflecting luminous blues, oranges, and purples. Clavity checked his watch. Perhaps he had the wrong time? Or even the wrong day? He sighed and looked around for something to read.

'Ah, Major. Thank you for your patience,' said a voice from the doorway.

A tall, thin figure with silvery-grey hair walked into the office and closed the door. He hung a dusty trench coat on a stand and took off a wide-brimmed hat.

'I'm sorry to keep you waiting, Major. An urgent matter came to light.'

Clavity shifted uneasily in his seat and stood up. He was unsure whether to shake hands or salute. He decided on the latter and stood to attention.

'Reporting as requested, sir.'

Olandis smiled.

'There's no need for formalities here, Major. Please relax.'

Clavity did as he was told.

'You wanted to see me, Founder?'

Olandis sat on a leather couch facing him.

'I've transferred you to my personal staff for an important mission.'

'How can I help, sir?' said Clavity, his heart pounding.

A pair of silver eyes twinkled in his direction.

'I can see you're nervous, Major. You're wondering why you've been chosen and why you're here? First, I need you to believe in your abilities, Major Charles Nathaniel Clavity.'

Clavity felt a warm glow inside his chest and trembled. The warmth spread and waves of energy swept through his body. His eyes told him there were two Founders; then three; then four. They all sat on the couch, watching him with glistening eyes and confident smiles. Visions raced through his mind. He watched his hands assemble unusual equipment in the middle of a woods, while he stood, guarding a ruined building. When he woke from his trance, Clavity realised he was facing a solitary figure.

'Do you have any questions?' said Olandis.

Clavity spoke at pace and caught up with his words after they had left his mouth.

'What is the purpose of my mission?'

'I need you to make preparations for me. You will be my eyes and ears.'

'But why me?' said Clavity, blushing when he realised what he had said.

'Because your spirit is brave and honest. And I need you to protect me.'

'I thought you already had bodyguards?'

Olandis stood and smiled.

'You don't miss anything, do you?'

Two ghostly shapes appeared in the corners of the room. They wore identical pinstriped suits and orange-tinted sunglasses.

'Put it this way, Major, there's an assassin coming for me, and even my bodyguards will be powerless when it chooses to strike.'

Speechless, Clavity watched the bodyguards blend into the corners of the room.

'If you'll excuse me, Major? I'll be in touch again very soon.'

'Yes, sir!' said Clavity, standing to attention.

****

Rusham slithered and splashed her way through a dense woods. A heavy backpack dug into her shoulders, and she winced with every step. She followed a line of commando cadets on a muddy trail around trees, upended roots, and bushes.

'Yuck!' she said, treading in a pile of animal droppings.

While she wiped her boot on a pile of leaves, it occurred to Rusham that the training exercise was pointless. Her team had walked through the rain for hours, and her feet were aching. They were now hopelessly lost.

The cadets reached a small clearing, and evening sunlight cast a golden glow on the treetops. Birds chirped, and trees rustled in a light breeze. The clearing was covered in dense ferns and leaf litter. If they were lucky, there would be another hour of daylight.

'We'll pitch camp here,' said Sergeant Briggs.

He sent cadets running to fetch wood, stones, and branches. He ordered Cadets Rusham and Hawkes to take first watch, while their colleagues lit a fire and set up camp. Rusham felt relieved until the rain returned.

A loud clattering noise filled the air, scattering birds and sending leaves flying. An engine thundered overhead, and a camouflaged figure abseiled into the clearing. Sergeant Briggs ran across and saluted the new arrival.

'Squad, attenshun!' cried Briggs. 'Listen up, cadets. This is Captain Ayres, who will command the rest of your training exercise.'

'It will be my pleasure to train you in fieldcraft,' said Ayres. 'Over the next two weeks, you will trap your own food and fend for yourselves in this woods. Are there any questions?'

'What in heaven's name am I doing here?' thought Rusham, as rainwater trickled down her neck.

****

When Sean woke the next morning, there was no sign of the cat. He walked down the creaky main staircase and noticed a colourful, stained glass window high above. It displayed the same crest he had seen on his fireplace. However, in the pale morning light, it looked like an eagle in flight. Sean was still craning his neck upwards as he crossed the hallway and tripped over a pile of bags.

'Ahh!' he cried, landing heavily on the tiled floor.

While Sean lay rubbing a sore hip, Mrs Campbell called to him from the corridor.

'Are you alright, my love? Emily, go and help Sean, will you? And please move your camping gear before someone breaks their neck.'

Sean watched a blonde-haired girl march down the corridor towards him. She gave an embarrassed smile.

'I'm ever so sorry. Are you okay? You must be Sean?'

Sean took her hand and rose gingerly to his feet.

'It's my camping gear. I came home late last night. I'm Emily, by the way. Pleased to meet you.'

'Hi,' said Sean, shaking her hand.

Emily had a kind face and long, fair hair. Two strands were braided in a Roman style and joined on the back of her head like a regal tribute. She was taller than Sean and a little older.

'Have you seen the crest on that window?' said Sean.

Emily seemed confused for a moment and crossed the hallway to take a look.

'Oh, that old thing?' she said. 'They're all over the house. According to the legend, they're hundreds of years old.'

Sean carried a sleeping bag and tent while Emily picked up her rucksack and muddy boots. Sean followed her to the kitchen.

'Where should we put these, Mum?' said Emily.

'In the scullery,' said Mrs Campbell. 'Next to the shoe rack.'

'What legend?' said Sean.

They deposited the equipment on the scullery floor and washed their hands in a porcelain saddle sink.

'I'll tell you over breakfast,' said Emily. 'And afterwards, I'll show you the well.'

'Well?' said Sean.

'Very well, thank you,' said Emily, grinning. 'Actually, there's a spring under the main building. It's why they built the manor here.'

While Sean wolfed down his porridge and hot chocolate, Emily told the story of Kimbleton Hall. It began in ancient times when a Bronze Age tribe buried their treasure on a hillside near a spring. It was discovered centuries later by monks who built a small monastery near the site and dug a fishpond. The monks were fearful of the treasure's power and kept it hidden in their cellar for hundreds of years. The monastery was destroyed in a fire, and the treasure was forgotten. Many years later, a hunting lodge was built on the site, and the new owner of Kimbleton Hall discovered it while constructing a wine cellar. He went mad and led his family into ruin.

Mrs Campbell raised her eyebrows.

'It's a load of old nonsense if you ask me. Kimbleton Hall was a country retreat for a wealthy family. The Lord of the Manor gambled away their fortune, and the Foundation bought it for a song.'

'But what about the treasure?' said Sean. 'Has anyone ever found it?'

Emily shook her head.

'Some people think it was reburied in the woods.'

'If you ask me, it doesn't exist,' said Mrs Campbell. 'Are you full, Sean? Help yourself to some toast, dear.'

A face peered around the dining room door and just as quickly vanished.

'Who was that?' said Emily.

'Maya, the new maid,' said Mrs Campbell.

'She looks creepy,' said Emily, to Sean's amusement.

'Don't be rude, Emily! I need the help. I've been rushed off my feet.'

'Come on, Sean, I'll show you the well,' said Emily.

'Be careful down there,' said Mrs Campbell.

Sean followed Emily to a utility room cupboard, where she collected a torch.

'How long are you going to stay with us?'

'I don't know,' said Sean. 'The council demolished our house, and now we've nowhere to live.'

'That's awful! And where are your parents?'

'Mum is away visiting an aunt.'

'And your dad?'

'I don't remember him.'

'Why? What happened?'

'Mum told me he's missing in action,' said Sean.

'For the Foundation?'

'I think so. She doesn't like to talk about it.'

Emily closed the cupboard.

'So you could be here for a while?'

Sean nodded. He noticed Emily wore a silver necklace shaped like a crescent moon.

'Did you hurt your arm?' said Emily, glancing at Sean's bandage.

'Yeah, it's a long story. It's still a bit sore.'

'Promise you'll tell me? Mum said it was on the news.'

'I guess,' said Sean.

'This way.'

Emily lifted a latch and opened a rickety, wooden door. Behind it were steps leading down. She clicked on a light switch and led the way.

'Use the handrail. It's very steep.'

After a slow descent, they reached a small room with a low, vaulted ceiling. A single light bulb dangled overhead. Built into the far wall was a row of metal wine racks. Otherwise, the room was empty.

'Are there any ghosts down here?' said Sean, hearing his voice echo.

'I've never met one. The well is over here,' said Emily, switching on her torch.

The ceiling curved above them into a series of vaulted arches, each supported by a pillar where two arches met. The pillars formed a row of passageways, which stretched under the house. One side was sectioned off into a storage room by rusty metal railings.

'What's in there?' said Sean.

'I don't know. It's locked.'

They snaked left and right under the house and reached a dead end.

'That's odd,' said Emily, pointing her torch at a solid wall.

'What's wrong?'

'This isn't how I remembered it. The passage used to go

under the oldest part of the house.'

On closer examination, one side of the wall was made of mouldy stone, and the other was smooth brick. An archway had been recently filled in.

'I think the well is on the other side of this wall,' said Emily, tapping the brickwork.

Emily's torch faded and died.

'Hey, what's going on?' she said, shaking it.

'Dead batteries?' said Sean.

They stood in total darkness and listened to the sound of running water.

'What was that?' said Emily.

'Water in the pipes, I guess?'

Sean edged forwards in the pitch black. It was so dark he could not even see his hand in front of his face.

'I don't know how we're going to find our way out.'

'Don't go anywhere; I'm scared of the dark,' said Emily, her voice quivering.

Sean took Emily's hand. He led her towards the cellar wall and felt his way along it. They made slow progress. After a few tentative steps, Sean trod on something hard and rolled it under his sneaker. He reached down and picked it up. It felt cold and rounded like a large, metal fountain pen.

'What are you doing?' said Emily.

'I've found something.'

'Is it a torch?'

'I don't think so,' said Sean, running his fingers over the cylinder and probing for a switch.

Sean slipped it into his pocket, and an idea came to him.

'Watch, alive.'

At once, the timepiece displayed 10:26 in bright numerals.

'Watch, light on.'

A ring of blue light shone from his watch. It only carried a short distance, but it was bright enough to see where they were going. Emily gripped his hand, and they rounded a corner. As they did so, a pair of bright circles flashed in front of them.

‘Ahhh!’ cried Emily, hiding behind Sean.

Sean felt a knot in his stomach. What could it be? An androbot? He pointed the watch at the circles. They moved closer and became larger and larger. Soon, a face appeared out of the gloom. It was white and covered in ginger stripes.

‘What are you doing down here?’ said the cat.

‘Exploring,’ said Sean.

‘Who said that?’ said Emily, cowering behind him.

‘My cat.’

‘You have a *talking* cat?’ said Emily. ‘Pull the other one!’

‘Say something, Tiger.’

The cat rubbed its tail against Sean’s leg and stalked off into the murky cellar.

‘Tiger’s gone, remember?’ said a voice in Sean’s head. ‘Nice try, Einstein.’

‘This way,’ said Sean. ‘This creepy cat will lead us out of here.’

Emily followed, still gripping Sean’s hand.

‘I thought you said your cat could talk?’

‘Yeah, well, it’s not my cat,’ said Sean.

‘And less of the creepy,’ said a voice in his head.

CHAPTER 9: DISCOVERIES

Sean and Emily were grateful to see daylight again and picked cobwebs from their hair. By the time they had recovered, the cat had disappeared.

'Where have you two been?' said Mrs Campbell. 'Mr Steele's waiting for you in the morning room.'

'Huh?' said Sean, brushing dust from his trousers.

'You have lessons this morning,' said Mrs Campbell.

'But, Mum!' said Emily.

'Sorry, dear, you both need to attend. Follow me.'

Sean and Emily grumbled as they walked. Mrs Campbell took them through several doors to a room on the far side of the East Wing. She knocked at a wood-panelled door and ushered them inside.

'See you later, my dears.'

'Ah, my eager young students,' said a serious-looking man, with bushy eyebrows and extra-thick glasses.

He invited them into a yellow morning room, which had sunlight streaming in through two bay windows. There were rugs on the floor and a pair of crystal chandeliers. A white screen covered the far wall, and a large wooden globe stood in the middle of the room. Steele waved Sean and Emily to a pair of school desks.

'Welcome. My name is Mr Steele. Shall we make a start?'

'On what?' said Sean, rolling the globe under his hand.

'Your instruction, of course.'

'But I go to Somerstead School,' said Emily. 'And term doesn't start until next Wednesday.'

'Ah, I see,' said Steele, closing the door. 'Where shall we begin?'

'After the rest of my holiday?' said Emily.

Steele wore a concerned expression and strode towards them in a pair of squeaky, brown shoes.

'I'm sorry, Emily, but you will not be returning to your old school.'

'Why not?' said Emily, horrified. 'What about my friends?'

'It would be far too dangerous. There's a significant risk you'd be followed and kidnapped.'

'And what about my school?' said Sean.

Steele sighed and gave a pained look.

'Hasn't anyone explained *anything* to you? I suppose you haven't done your homework either?'

Emily grimaced.

'What homework?'

'You mean that *weird* book?' said Sean.

'Yes, Sean, that weird book,' said Steele. 'Can you both take a seat, please?'

Sean and Emily exchanged rebellious smirks and stayed on their feet.

'Sit!' said Steele, his eyes glowering.

Sean looked at Steele's face. He did not appear to be angry, but Sean felt compelled to do as he was told. He found himself sitting behind a wooden, flip-top desk and watched Emily do the same.

'Good. Now, if there's any fuss, I'll have to give you both detention,' said Steele.

'But this *is* detention,' thought Sean.

'Yes, I suppose this lesson may seem like detention in a way,' said Steele, returning to his desk. 'But it's far better than being attacked by Krankhausen, wouldn't you agree, Sean?'

He felt a cold chill.

'I can also hear your thoughts,' said a voice in Sean's head. 'In case you were wondering.'

Steele raised his right hand and clicked his fingers.

'Watch closely.'

The globe revolved and split along a central line. Its hemispheres separated and slid around each other to form a bowl-like shape. They revealed a small crystal pyramid lying on a black, polished slab. Beams of light leaped from the pyramid and projected the head and shoulders of a bearded man with dark hair. His torso rotated, and Sean recognised his face.

'This is Egbert Von Krankhausen,' said Steele. 'He's stolen billions in gold, oil, and gemstones from around the world. He's also responsible for thousands of deaths, including several Foundation staff.'

The projection changed to show a pale-faced man with red eyes and white hair.

'This is Darius Deveraux. We understand he's been funding Krankhausen's operation for a considerable time. Deveraux has not been seen by anyone for over three years. He is believed to be one of the richest people alive.'

'I don't understand,' said Sean.

'About why this matters to you?'

Sean gave a nod.

'These men are trying you capture you, Sean. It appears they want you alive, which is fortunate.'

Sean felt a shiver run down his spine. Emily reached out and held his hand.

'And anyone close to you is also at risk,' said Steele. 'Sorry, Emily.'

'It's not your fault,' said Emily, giving a consoling smile. 'But *why* do these men want Sean? What's he ever done to them?'

Steele took a deep breath and pointed a device at the pyramid. The hologram changed into three colourful ladders spiralling around each other.

'They want this.'

'What is it?' said Emily.

'This is a picture of Sean's DNA. His genetic imprint, if you like. This is what makes Sean who he is. We believe Krankhausen and Deveraux intend to create a clone army using Sean's DNA,' said Steele.

'What's a clone?' said Sean.

'A clone is a genetic copy. Do you remember those creatures who attacked you at Yeatsford?'

Sean nodded.

'They were identical, bio-mechanical clones.'

'Sorry?' said Sean.

'Androbots - part human and part machine.'

'But why would anyone want to clone Sean?' said Emily.

Steele smiled and took off his glasses.

'Because he's gifted, Emily. You may not yet realize it, Sean, but you have some rare abilities. Which is why the Foundation has been protecting you all these years.'

'Do you mean the dreams?' said Sean.

Steele glanced at him for a moment and closed his eyes as if meditating.

'Hmm, fascinating. Now then, shall we crack on?'

Sean and Emily pulled faces.

'History. Who can tell me why Kimbleton Hall was built on this site?'

****

Darius Deveraux tapped an enormous glass vat containing bubbling liquid and a gelatinous blob. He inspected a row of dials, and his expression became stern.

'Hurry it up, Seventy-one. Time is of the essence.'

'Master, the Constructor has already completed its task.'

'Then where are the creatures I ordered?'

'A landing party took them ashore this morning.'

'To Kimbleton Woods?' said Deveraux.

'Yes, master.'

'And why wasn't I informed?'

'You were asleep, master. The landing party will release our spy-bots into Kimbleton Woods as you instructed.'

Deveraux turned to his second-in-command and smiled.

'Good work, Seventy-one. We'll make a man of you yet.'

'A *man*, master?' said the androbot.

'Just my little joke, Seventy-one. No need to look so hurt,' said Deveraux, patting him on the shoulder.

The androbot remained impassive and stared into space.

'Oh, never mind,' said Deveraux, heading to his quarters. 'Let me know when our spy-bots are active.'

'Yes, master,' said Seventy-one, following in his footsteps and treading on his heels.
'Do you mind?' said Deveraux, entering a toilet cubicle and locking the door behind him.

****

Sean and Emily returned to the dining room for a lunch of roast chicken and vegetables.
'Tell me about these gifts of yours,' said Emily.
'What do you mean?'
'You know, the abilities Steele was talking about?'
'Oh, it's nothing. Sometimes I have strange dreams.'
'Go on?'
Sean took a mouthful of food and shrugged.
'I'm waiting,' said Emily, rolling her eyes. 'I'm missing all my friends because of these *abilities* of yours.'
Sean swallowed hard.
'I can sometimes hear voices in my dreams.'
'And?' said Emily, looking unimpressed. 'Those creeps want to clone you because you can hear voices?'
'I guess,' said Sean, eyeing his food.
'What else can you do?' said Emily, pushing carrots around her plate.
Mrs Campbell wandered in and noticed Emily's food was untouched.
'Hurry up, you two. I'll be clearing the table in a couple of minutes. You need to get some fresh air.'
'Yes, Mum,' said Emily, pretending to eat some vegetables.
Mrs Campbell returned to the kitchen.
'Well?'
Sean wrinkled his forehead.
'Sometimes I know when something bad is about to happen.'
'Like the time you went shopping?'
'Yeah, sort of. But it doesn't always work.'
Emily smiled and poured herself a glass of water. Sean

curled his lip.

'What's the matter?'

'I need to go,' said Sean, leaving the table.

'Where to?'

'I'll be back in a moment.'

Sean hurried away in search of the nearest cloakroom. He raced along the main corridor and tried a few doors. On his third attempt, he smelled bleach and locked the door behind him. In his haste, Sean tripped over a mat and stumbled forwards. He landed on his hands and knees in front of the toilet.

'Ouch!' he cried.

After answering the call of nature, Sean washed his hands and winced. His palms were sore. As he turned to leave, he kicked the bathroom mat and noticed something unusual. Set among the small, white tiles was a coloured pattern.

Sean rolled back the mat. Underneath it, he discovered a mosaic. It showed a pair of curved antlers, a circle underneath, and a shining star above. Or did it? Sean took a closer look and saw a shape like a beak and claws. Was it a bird carrying a ring? He noticed the glint of a square ridge running around the mosaic. It felt cold and smooth like metal.

'I wonder?' he whispered, running his fingers over the tiles.

Although the design was set in the floor, it felt rough and slightly raised. Sean spotted a metal ring held by the bird's talons and smiled.

****

Professor Quark arrived in an elevator on the first-floor of the Foundation's HQ. He clutched a small, metal briefcase against his chest and caught sight of a familiar figure ambling down the corridor. He hurried to catch up.

'Brigadier?'

'Ah, Professor. Is this a social call?'

'Shall we go into your office?'

Cuthbertson's office was full of blueprints. The walls were covered in technical drawings, and his desk was hidden under a pile of paperwork. The blueprints showed every conceivable angle of a submarine in cross-section.

'I don't know how we're going to manage it,' muttered Cuthbertson.

'Manage what?'

'To build this submarine, of course. Not one of our shipyards has a clue.'

Quark stooped to read a blueprint.

'It looks pretty straightforward to me.'

'Yes,' said Cuthbertson. 'Until you consider the materials the Founder wants us to use.'

'And what are those?'

Cuthbertson handed him a sheet of paper listing chemical formulae and instructions for making metal alloys and polymers.

'We're going to need our own smelting plant and plastics factory,' said Quark. 'Can we afford all this?'

Cuthbertson sat at his desk and put his arms behind his head.

'All I know is the Founder has asked for quotations.'

Quark gave a concerned nod.

'Anyway, how can I help you?'

Quark took a seat and positioned the briefcase beside him.

'We've discovered the cause of our vehicle failures. We caught two miniature robots trying to break into the armoury.'

'Enemy robots inside the HQ? Impossible!' said Cuthbertson.

'If I may?' said Quark, gesturing to his briefcase.

Cuthbertson looked unimpressed.

'This is what's left of the first robot,' said Quark, tipping the contents of his briefcase onto Cuthbertson's desk.

Charred pieces of limbs, wires, and sensors scattered fell on a blueprint of the submarine's living quarters.

'Great Scott!' said Cuthbertson. 'What is it?'

Quark dangled a leg and antenna in front of Cuthbertson.

'We're calling it a spyder-bot. A creature related to the spider family. Arachnid if you prefer,' said Quark. 'But it's been altered.'

'In what way?' said Cuthbertson.

'Our analysis shows this is a mutated living organism connected to robotic parts. We found traces of computer chips and a transmitter in its remains.'

'Remains?'

'Yes, it self-destructed while we were dissecting it.'

Cuthbertson raised his eyebrows.

'Was anyone hurt?'

'No, we were lucky,' said Quark. 'We also examined the remains of the androbots who attacked Sean Yeager.'

'Who?'

'The boy we've been protecting? The target of the shoot-out at Yeatsford shopping centre?'

'Ah yes, it's coming back to me now. But we're all safe and sound now, aren't we?'

'Err, yes, Brigadier.'

'Excellent! I knew you were the man for the job.'

Before Quark could explain his concerns any further, a loud siren and flashing lights interrupted their meeting.

'Ye gads, what's that?' said Cuthbertson, leaping to his feet.

The two men reached for their phones and rang the control centre for information. Quark was quickest and reached the duty officer.

'Then seal it off! And get Reynard down there with an assault team.'

Cuthbertson put down his phone and turned to Quark for answers.

'One of the Yeatsford androbots is trying to break out of Laboratory-three.'

'Then what are you waiting for?' said Cuthbertson, waving him to the door.

Quark stood speechless for a moment, his heart pounding.
'Do I know you?' he thought.
'Keep me informed, Professor,' said Cuthbertson, with a smile. 'And switch off those pesky alarms, will you? They're hurting my ears.'

****

Reynard studied a screen flanked by a team of ten commandos. It showed a dark-suited figure hurling furniture at a glass cell wall inside Laboratory-three. The wall vibrated with every impact but held firm. The androbot stopped and raised its left hand. One of its fingers split open, and it extended a tool. It approached the cell door and tried to cut a hole around the lock and handle. When this failed, the androbot raised its right hand, and a red light shone from its index finger.
'What's it doing?' said one of the commandos.
'It looks like a laser cutter,' said Reynard. 'Control, flood the cell with nerve gas.'
'Confirmed, switching on the gas supply in three, two, one, now,' said the duty officer.
'Okay, team, put on your gas masks; we're going in,' said Reynard.
A fine white mist descended on the androbot. Despite the nerve gas, it continued to melt a circular hole in the door. The lock gave way, and with a kick, the androbot was free.
'Open fire!' said Reynard.
Bullets ricocheted off the cell wall, and the androbot dived and rolled for cover. It moved at incredible speed and ripped a small workbench from the floor. Using the bench as a shield, it charged at the nearest commandos and ran through them. The androbot crashed into the laboratory door and bounced off it.
'Switch blasters to electro-bolts!' said Reynard.
The commandos regrouped and aimed their weapons at the androbot. It raised its right arm and extended its palm as

if to surrender. The team hesitated for a split second, and a volley of darts flew across the room. One pierced a commando's facemask and embedded itself a fraction from his forehead.

'Fire!' cried Reynard.

A hail of electro-bolts leaped through the air and struck the androbot. Blue sparks rippled across its chest and limbs, making it twitch and stagger. Its legs gave way, and it slumped to its knees.

'Cease fire!'

Before Reynard could reach the stricken creature, it began to melt. A white, frothing mush oozed from its body and spread across the floor.

'Get a medic in here!' cried Reynard, gesturing to the dart victim on the floor.

'What's your status, Captain?' said Quark on the intercom.

'We have three men down, and your lab is a mess.'

'And the androbot?'

'What's left of it is turning into soup.'

****

Clavity hummed a tune to himself while he worked in Kimbleton Woods. He unloaded cases from a Hovertrike and laid them in a circle around the ruins of an old stone cottage. It seemed like second nature, and he gave his work little thought. Each case contained a device the size of a dinner plate. Clavity activated one by flicking a switch and tapping in a code. Once its light flashed green, he laid it on the ground and covered it with a few dead leaves. He loaded the empty cases back onto the Hovertrike and smiled.

Relieved his work was done, Clavity stretched his back and shoulders. Something moved under a nearby bush, and he span around. He switched on his camouflage and scanned the area. Clavity saw nothing in the visible spectrum except for trees and bushes. On infrared, there was a tiny speck. Invisible, he crept forwards and drew his blaster. To his left, there was another rustle of leaves. Clavity knelt behind a fallen tree and fired. His weapon flashed and blew a pile of leaves into vapour. A tiny, brown bird appeared from behind the bush and flew away. Clavity chuckled to himself. Perhaps he was becoming trigger-happy in his old age? A loud squawk from the bird seemed to answer his question. Clavity flicked on the blaster's safety catch and rose.

****

A large, olive-green lizard crawled across a meadow on four stubby legs. It arched its back and flicked its tongue in the air. After a brief pause, it changed direction and scrambled under a barbed wire fence. It meandered through the undergrowth and passed a sign that read: *Strictly no entry. Trespassers will be prosecuted.*

'Master, we are about to enter Kimbleton Woods,' said Seventy-one.

'Show me,' said Deveraux.

They watched a scene of undergrowth being pushed aside. The camera moved under a fence and splashed through a ditch. It climbed a muddy bank and approached a line of trees. An instant later, the screen flashed and went blank.

'What happened?' said Deveraux.

'We've lost our spy-bot, master.'

'Did you order it to tunnel into the woods?'

'No, master.'

'Typical! What did I tell you about force fields? Deploy the rest of our spy-bots. And this time, make sure they dig their way in or fly over the trees!'

'It will be done, master.'

CHAPTER 10: SEARCH PARTY

Brawne scanned Kimbleton Hall's driveway through his office window. He expected Hughes to return at any minute and drummed his fingers on the windowsill. According to his superiors, Hughes had been found alive and well at the Luke Harris department store. He had evaded capture by prising open the base of a display cabinet and crawling under the floor. Unfortunately for Hughes, he had then become wedged between two floor supports, and it took a day to release him.

A blacked-out people carrier hurried along the driveway and pulled up outside. Brawne strode down the servant's corridor. He emerged beside the main door and stepped outside to greet the new arrivals. A solitary figure alighted from the vehicle.

'Mr Hughes, I'm glad to see you're alive and well.'

'Yes, sir. The medics gave me a clean bill of health.'

'I'm glad to hear it. From what I heard, you were in a tight spot?'

'Yes, sir. We had a few awkward customers to deal with.'

Brawne looked him up and down.

'Are you feeling well enough for duty?'

'I'm a little creaky but otherwise okay.'

'Excellent. The outer defence barrier has developed another fault, and no one else has a clue how to fix it. Can you check it out?'

Hughes straightened and smiled.

'Sure, no problem. Whereabouts?'

'Between marker-32 and 33,' said Brawne. 'You can take my quad bike.'

'Right away, sir.'

It was rare for Brawne to offer anyone his quad bike, and Hughes could not believe his luck. He hurried back to his quarters and put on his fatigues and boots before Brawne changed his mind. On his way to the garage, Hughes collected a toolkit and controller from the guardhouse. He checked his communicator was fully charged and secured the equipment to a map holder in front of the quad bike's handlebars. He started up its engine and set off.

Hughes followed a shingle track and approached a gate at the edge of the woods. He pressed a key on the controller and waited a few seconds. The gate swung open, and he rumbled through. Before entering the woods, Hughes stopped and threw a stone at the barrier. It sailed through unscathed. Satisfied he was not about to be fried, he drove on and re-activated the force field behind him.

The woods was aglow with breathtaking shades of red, orange, and yellow. All around him, trees prepared for their winter rest. It was tough going, and Hughes wrestled the quad bike through several long stretches of mud and puddles, spraying dirt everywhere. Kimbleton Woods covered three thousand acres, but marker-32 was only a mile away. It was said that the woods used to be a royal hunting ground, and herds of deer still roamed free. While negotiating some deep ruts, Hughes considered the possible causes of the barrier's fault. Perhaps a deer had ignored the ultra-sonic alarm and run into it? Or maybe an energy coupling had burned out? He rode on and admired the scenery as rabbits and squirrels darted away in search of cover.

****

Sean rattled along the length of the library wall on a set of wheeled steps. He raced past rows of books that were packed into shelves from floor to ceiling.

'What are you doing?' said Emily.

'Looking for a book.'

'Come on, slowcoach. I want to get this homework over and done with.'

'What do we have to do again?' said Sean, squeaking to a halt.

'Weren't you listening?'

'All I heard was: blah, blah, blah, history of Kimbleton Hall.'

'Don't let Steele hear you say that,' said Emily. 'Or we'll both be in detention!'

'Aren't we already? It's like a prison in here.'

Emily sighed. She missed her school friends, and the idea of being tutored at home was not appealing.

'I almost forgot,' said Sean, jumping down from the steps. 'I found something in the downstairs cloakroom.'

'I *do not* want to know!' said Emily.

Sean frowned.

'No, not *that*. I found a crest on the floor.'

'How exciting?' said Emily. 'They're all over the house, haven't you noticed?'

Sean looked hurt.

'Sorry,' said Emily. 'It's the crest of the De Beaufort family. They built most of the house.'

'Most of it?'

'Yes. According to this book, they built it over the ruins of the old monastery.'

'Okay, smartypants, so why is there a manhole in the cloakroom?'

Emily burst out laughing.

'What's so funny?'

'Isn't it obvious? It *is* a cloakroom.'

After several minutes of giggling, Sean and Emily managed to steady themselves.

'And what's so special about this *manhole* of yours?' said Emily, wiping her eyes.

Sean took a deep breath to stifle his laughter.

'I think it leads to the cellar.'

'And the well!' said Emily, rising from her chair.

'What about our homework?'

'It can wait a few minutes, can't it?'

****

Hughes reached one edge of the woods and swept a scanner in the direction of a meadow. It remained silent, and there was no trace of the defence barrier. He climbed off the quad bike and approached marker-32. The body of a dead animal lay beside a force field projector.

'Hughes to Bird's Nest. Come in, Bird's Nest.'

'Brawne here. What is it, Hughes?'

'Take a look at this, sir. On camera now.'

'Ye gads! What is it?' said Brawne.

Hughes poked a long stick in the creature's belly and rolled it over with his boot.

'Looks like a barbied croc to me, sir.'

'A what?'

'A barbecued reptile,' said Hughes. 'A big one too.'

'Where did it come from?'

'Beats me,' said Hughes.

'Can you repair the barrier?'

'I think so. It looks like it shorted out when it roasted this reptile. I'll check the distributor grid.'

'Right away, Hughes. I need that barrier working again as soon as possible.'

'Yes, sir!' said Hughes, happy to be busy again.

****

Emily knelt over the floor mosaic and rifled through her pockets. She produced a plastic pen lid and wriggled it under the cover's brass ring. She pulled upwards and the pen lid snapped.

'You're right; it *is* a manhole. And I bet it leads to the cellar. But how do we lift it?'

'Here, let me have a go,' said Sean.

They took turns trying to raise the brass ring until their fingers were sore. However, the manhole cover refused to budge.

'We need something to lever it open,' said Sean.

'Like what?'

'Something long, I guess.'

'I know,' said Emily, rushing off.

'And a torch that works?' said Sean, wandering after her.

In the corridor, Sean met the cat. It raised its tail and prowled towards him.

'What are you doing here? Was studying too exciting for you?'

Sean tried to look casual.

'Oh, nothing. Just waiting for the cloakroom.'

The cat tilted its head from side to side.

'I can tell you're lying, Sean. What are you really up to?'

Sean sighed.

'If you must know, it's smelly in there, and neither of us can open the window.'

The cat narrowed its eyes and scanned Sean from head to toe.

'And what's that in your pocket?'

'Something I found it in the cellar,' said Sean, producing a plain, metal cylinder. 'Any idea what it is?'

The cat sniffed the metal tube.

'It's a standard-issue, Foundation micro-cutter. You need to hand it over to Mr Steele right away.'

'How does it work?' said Sean, running his fingers over its ridged, metal casing.

'Like I'm going to let you loose with a dangerous weapon? No way, kiddo,' said the cat. 'Anyway, it's deactivated.'

'Mind if I keep it?' said Sean, putting the micro-cutter back in his pocket.

'No, Sean…' said the cat, startled by the approach of footsteps

Emily appeared, followed by Braveheart. The cat hissed in disgust and bared its teeth. Braveheart barked and ran off, pursued by Emily.

'What you are doing?'

'It's my programming. And if her dog comes sniffing my butt again, I'll laser its ears off!'

Before the cat could question him any further, Emily came charging down the corridor waving a broom.

'Shoo! You wicked beast!'

'Yikes!' said the cat, fleeing the scene.

Emily chased it out of the house and across the driveway. She returned several minutes later, panting.

'Sorry about that,' said Sean.

'Your cat gives me the creeps.'

'You do realise it's not mine?'

'Then why is it here?'

Sean looked thoughtful.

'It's wasn't my idea that's for sure. I wanted a dog, but our house was too small.'

When Emily had recovered her breath, they returned to the cloakroom and locked the door. After much scraping and heaving, the manhole cover came loose. They dragged it across the floor and revealed the top of a narrow, spiral staircase.

'Did you bring a torch?' said Sean.

'Of course,' said Emily, smirking. 'Come on! We don't have long 'til dinner.'

Emily inched down the first flight of steps. It was a tight squeeze.

'Lean to the outside,' said Sean, remembering his day trips to ruined castles.

The steps led down to a passage, which had a low ceiling and smelled of damp. After a few paces, they came to a half-open door covered in rusty, metal studs.

'This is it!' said Emily, examining the doorway with her torch.

Sean wrestled the door open. Beyond it was a room containing a waist-high, circular wall covered by a metal grille.

'And is this the well?' said Sean, rattling the grille.

'Sure is. There used to be a hand pump here as well.'

'What's that?' said Sean, pointing to a corner.

Emily's torch picked out a metal bollard that stood alone among the shadows. On the opposite side of the room was another wooden door. Sean tapped a knuckle against the bollard. It was solid, rounded, and firmly rooted to the floor.

'Any clues?' said Emily.

'It's like something you'd find at a car park.'

'But what's it doing here?'

Sean gave a shrug.

'Guarding the entrance?'

Sean tried to wrench the second door open. It shook from top to bottom but remained resolutely locked.

'I wonder where this leads.'

'What do your *abilities* tell you?' said Emily.

'To open it and find out.'

'I dare you.'

'And I dare you to come with me *when* I open it.'

'It's a deal. But look at the lock; it's covered in rust,' said Emily, shining her torch over the door handle.

Sean borrowed the torch and scoured the room for a key. However, there was only a row of empty hooks on the wall, and the rest of the room was bare. He tried turning the door handle and discovered it was wedged tight. Sean was about to give up when he noticed the door frame was rotten. If only he had something to prise it open?

'We need to get back,' said Emily.

'Watch, alive. Laser, alive,' said Sean, pointing his wrist at the door frame. A bright red light shone from the edge of his watch.

'Hey, what are you doing?' said Emily, stepping back.

'Cutting around the lock.'

Sparks cascaded onto the floor, and Sean cut a deep groove into the door frame.

'Laser, off,' said Sean.

'Where did you get that watch?' said Emily.

'Major Clavity gave it to me.'

Sean pulled the handle again. This time part of the door frame splintered and gave way. The door revealed another dark tunnel that stretched away into the distance.

'Are you coming? Or are you a scaredy-cat?'

****

Professor Quark removed a motionless spyder-bot from the jaws of a Marauder Class prowler. He sealed it inside a transparent plastic cube and placed it on a workbench. He was nervous after witnessing the androbot's rampage in Laboratory-three and made a series of quick decisions.

'Fullbright, I want all the androbot remains in Lab-three incinerated.'

'I'll see to it personally, Professor.'

'And then I want their ashes frozen, compressed into a block, and placed in a containment field.'

'Yes, sir. And what about this spyder-bot?'

'I'll cook this one myself.'

He carried the motionless spyder-bot on a tray to an adjoining room. It was a cramped space containing an impressive white device covered in coils and wires. Quark removed the spyder-bot from its cube and locked it inside a chamber. He slammed a heavy door behind him and returned to the main laboratory.

'Let's see how you like *this*,' he said, setting the machine's controls on a computer screen.

From the safety of Laboratory-one, Quark blasted the spyder-bot with enough radiation to cook the Foundation's meals for a week. When the radiation gun had cooled down, he retrieved the spyder-bot in two gloved hands and dropped it into a drum of liquid nitrogen.

'Welcome to freeze-land!'

A cloud of gas and bubbles erupted and spilled over the sides of the drum. Quark used a metal claw to remove the frozen spyder-bot and carried it to a glass, biohazard tank. He sealed it back inside its cube and secured the tank's airlock. Before leaving the laboratory, Quark trained cameras on the spyder-bot and activated a security system.

'One move, and we'll blast you into dust,' he said, chuckling all the way back to his office.

Several hours later, a cloud of condensation started to form inside the cube. Molecule by molecule, the spyder-bot began to defrost, and a faint red light flickered on.

****

Sean borrowed Emily's torch and took a few tentative steps into the tunnel. It was carved out of chalky soil with tree roots and pieces of flint suspended in its walls and ceiling. Its floor was covered in puddles and reminded Sean of a school caving trip.

'Is this tunnel part of the legend?' he said, leading the way.

'You tell me. Can you smell treasure?'

'What treasure?'

Emily laughed.

'Were you listening to a thing I said?'

'Oh, *that* treasure.'

'Is there another?'

Sean ducked to avoid a cobweb and felt something scuttle past his feet.

'What was that?' said Emily.

'I think it was a rat.'

'Yuck!' cried Emily, grabbing Sean's arm and hiding behind him.

'Or a mouse,' said Sean.

'Eww!'

'Perhaps even a vole?'

'You have no idea, do you?'

'Either way, it's gone. Which means there must be another way out of here.'

'Spiders!' cried Emily, brushing a cobweb from her face.

'You're not afraid of them *as well*, are you?'

'Of course not. That would be silly.'

They splashed along the passage for several minutes before reaching a stone archway and daylight.

'We've made it,' said Sean.

'You still haven't told me about the treasure?'

Around them, treetops of all shapes and sizes reflected the last rays of sunshine, and an orange glow silhouetted the uppermost branches. Squirrels and birds darted around searching for food while a gentle mist gathered deep in the woods.

'Boom!'

Sean and Emily turned around in dread. A heavy blast door had sealed the tunnel entrance. Sean gave it a thump, but there was no sign of a handle or an opening mechanism.

'Fantastic!' said Emily. 'Now we're stuck out here. You and your stupid dare!'

A light drizzle began to fall, and Sean felt his stomach clench.

'It's okay. We just need to follow the tunnel back to the house.'

'And which way is that, genius?' said Emily, her hands on her hips.

They stood in a hollow at the bottom of a steep bank. Sean shook his head.

'The rear of the house faces south, and the sun sets in the west so, err…'

Emily raised her eyes to the heavens.

'Doesn't your watch have a compass?'

'Good idea,' said Sean. 'But first, we need to climb a tree to get a signal.'

'You *are* joking?'

****

Mrs Campbell had begun to prepare dinner in the kitchen. It seemed very quiet, so she went to check on Sean and Emily's progress. The library was empty. On her return to the kitchen, she met Hughes in the main corridor.

'Hello, James. How are you?'

'Pretty good, thanks. I don't suppose you could rustle me up a quick sandwich?'

'Of course, my dear,' said Mrs Campbell. 'Have you seen Sean and Emily on your travels?'

Hughes shook his head.

'I've only just come back from the woods. Why?'

'I left them in the library, doing their homework, and now they've vanished.'

'Have you checked their rooms?' said Hughes.

'I was upstairs only a few minutes ago, making their beds.'

'What was their homework about?'

'It was research about the house, I think.'

Hughes hurried to the library and found a pile of open maps and books. He came back wearing a deep frown.

'They could be anywhere. Wait here and call the guardhouse if they turn up.'

He stepped out into the corridor and clicked on his earpiece.

'Hughes to Bird's Nest. Come in, Bird's Nest.'

'Go ahead, Hughes,' said the guardhouse.

'Call out the guard! Sean and Emily have gone missing. We need to search the house and grounds immediately.'

'You're kidding? Brawne will blow his top.'

'I'm afraid he will.'

****

Sean and Emily trampled through fallen leaves, looking for a way to climb out of the hollow. The ground became uneven, and they made slow progress. Eventually, they found a deer trail and weaved around fallen branches and tree trunks. In the distance, the sun began to fade.

'And now we're lost!' said Emily.

'But we're heading north,' said Sean. 'The house must be in this direction.'

They trudged on until they reached level ground. The trees and bushes thinned out, and there was a meadow on the other side of a tall, mesh fence.

'We've made it,' said Emily.

'Stop!' said Sean. 'Don't move!'

'Why not?'

Sean threw a stick at the fence. It span through the air and vanished in a flash of brilliant, blue light several feet short of the wire mesh. Emily froze in horror.

'That could have been me!'

'It's a force field,' said Sean. 'I knew there was a reason Hughes wouldn't bring us into the woods.'

'How did you know it was there?'

'Something felt wrong.'

Emily looked perturbed and tilted her head to one side.

'Can you hear something?'

'I can hear *you*.'

'Very funny. No, a buzzing sound like bees.'

Sean's eyes grew wide in anticipation.

'Perhaps it's a search party?'

Moments later, a large, flying insect emerged from the trees. The size of a small bird, it had a metallic turquoise body, a black leathery head, and two pairs of blurred wings. It was joined by a formation of similar creatures.

'Dragonflies?' said Emily. 'But they're enormous!'

'Run!' said Sean, grabbing a stick from the ground.

The swarm of dragonflies changed direction and flew after them.

****

Darius Deveraux studied a map inside a cramped navigation room. He was interrupted by Seventy-one.

'We have located Sean Yeager, master.'

'Show me.'

The androbot led its master to a screen showing a boy and girl running between trees in a misty woods.

'Tag Yeager and mobilize our androbots,' said Deveraux. 'I want him captured by morning.'

'It will be done, master. And what about the girl?'

'She is of no consequence to our mission.'

CHAPTER 11: CAPTURE

The guardhouse office echoed to the sound of Brawne barking out orders.

'I want Sean and Emily found in the next hour! This building is meant to be under 24-hour surveillance. How in blazes have they disappeared? I want the house and grounds searched from top to bottom. Bring in sniffer dogs if you have to, but find them!'

The guards filed out grumbling and gathered their equipment.

'Happy days,' said Hughes, returning to the library.

Mrs Campbell confronted him.

'You don't think someone's kidnapped them do you?'

'I doubt it. Intruders would have set off the alarms.'

Hughes studied the books Emily and Sean had been reading. His earpiece vibrated. It was Brawne, and he stepped away from Mrs Campbell in case it was bad news.

'Hughes here. Go ahead, sir.'

'Someone used the escape tunnel to enter the woods. We detected an impact with the defence barrier soon afterwards.'

'Do we have any video footage, sir?'

'Unfortunately not. However, we think it was Sean and Emily. And it looks like they walked straight into the barrier.'

'I'll get a team down there right away.'

'Prepare for the worst. Take a medical kit and blaster,' said Brawne. 'I only hope we're not too late.'

Hughes turned to leave and found his path blocked by Mrs Campbell.

'Is it bad news?' she said in a trembling voice.

'I'm sure they're fine. I need to hot-tail it down there and bring them home.'

'I'd never forgive myself if anything's happened to them.'

'Don't worry, I'll have them back in time for supper,' said

Hughes. 'Mine's a ham salad sarnie, by the way.'

****

Sean and Emily ran until their lungs ached. They managed to keep the dragonflies at bay for several minutes. However, the deer trail became a muddy obstacle course, and they struggled to keep up the pace.

'They're gaining on us!' said Emily, untangling her jeans from a bramble bush.

'Keep running!' said Sean, wielding a long stick. 'I'll hold them off.'

The dragonflies arrived and hovered in formation over Sean's head. One by one, they dived at him. Sean swung his stick like a boy possessed. He struck the first and sent it spinning away into the undergrowth. The second buzzed him and turned to make another pass, and the third took the full force of his swing. Its wings collapsed in mid-flight, and Sean sent it sprawling into a bush.

The second dragonfly landed on his neck. Sean panicked and slapped it with his bare hand. He felt a sharp pain in his shoulder, and the insect dropped to the ground. Sean stamped on it and hurried away, clutching a bleeding wound. He ran after Emily, and the dragonflies followed in single file. A short while later, Sean found her panting beside a tree.

'We have to keep going.'

'I can't,' said Emily, clutching her stomach. 'I have a stitch.'

The dragonflies regrouped a few paces away, and Sean looked around for another weapon. There was a sudden flash of red light, and the lead dragonfly vanished in mid-air. In quick succession, two more shared its fate. Someone or something was protecting them. Sean and Emily armed themselves with more sticks, but the dragonflies retreated. There was a rustling to their left, and Sean noticed a tree trunk shimmer as if a blurred shape had passed by. It was followed by a faint crunch of leaves.

'Hey! Who's there?' cried Sean.

Emily glanced at him, her eyes wide.

'Thanks for helping us!'

There was no reply.

'Who do you think it was?' said Emily.

Sean shook his head.

'Whoever it was, I'm glad they're on our side.'

Emily noticed Sean was bleeding from his shoulder. She tried to examine his wound, but he backed away.

'It's nothing,' said Sean, dabbing at the cut with his shirt collar.

As they wandered deeper into the woods, a mist descended from the treetops. It was now almost too dark to see, and Sean switched on his watch light.

'Can you smell something?' he said, sniffing the air.

'Woodsmoke,' said Emily. 'We must be near a campfire.'

****

Clavity was bored. He had completed his task, and his orders were to watch and wait. To pass the time, he tested his communicator and tuned into Kimbleton Hall's frequency.

'All guards assemble at the South Gate. Wear your full combat gear,' said a voice on his earpiece. 'It is imperative we find Sean and Emily in the next hour. We believe they are somewhere in Kimbleton Woods.'

Clavity's heartbeat quickened, and he went to fetch his hoverpack.

'I could at least keep an eye on things from the air,' he mused.

****

Darius Deveraux strode down a narrow corridor and beckoned for Seventy-one to follow him. He was in a foul mood, but his second-in-command, as usual, failed to notice.

'It's time we introduced the Foundation to their demise.

Bring me Krankhausen.'

'Yes, master,' said Seventy-one, transmitting the order.

'And make sure we surround the house *and* woods. I will *not* have Yeager slipping through our fingers this time.'

'Master, we have three hundred androbots closing in.'

'Excellent. Keep me informed of their progress.'

Deveraux opened a bulkhead door with his palm print. In the next room, two androbots dragged Krankhausen to his feet. He looked drawn and weary.

'Egbert, how good of you to rouse yourself. I need to know more about the defences at Kimbleton Hall.'

'I, uh...' muttered Krankhausen, half asleep.

'As I thought. Prepare the mind probe, Seventy-one. This is going to hurt our guest considerably more than it's going to hurt me.'

****

Sean and Emily followed the aroma of burning wood like two bloodhounds. Sean's watch light was beginning to fade, and his shoulder ached. They made slow progress in the gathering gloom.

'I have a weird feeling about this woods,' said Sean.

'Great. And will your feelings warn us if we're about to be attacked again?'

Sean realised their predicament was his fault, and he blushed.

'I also have a strange feeling,' said Emily. 'It's like muddy water is filling up my shoes. And it's *very* realistic.'

'Sorry.'

'So, what now? Are we about to be savaged by a pack of wolves?'

'I think we're getting closer to the treasure.'

'How do you know?'

'I can hear the voices calling to me.'

They reached the edge of a clearing and squelched to a halt. Ahead of them, an open fire glowed in the mist. Beside it was the outline of a small hut.

'Well, it's not Kimbleton Hall,' whispered Sean.

'You don't say?'

'Shush, there's someone here.'

'You mean the fire didn't light itself?'

'Shhhh!'

A twig snapped to their right, and a figure approached carrying a bright lamp.

Sean and Emily backed away and almost tripped over a fallen branch.

'And what have we here?' said a deep voice. 'Two little foxes?'

Emily turned to run, but Sean caught her hand.

'Come on out, you two. You'll catch your death of cold out there,' said the stranger.

'Who are you?' said Sean.

'Come and warm yourselves by the fire. Names, always names. You know, I've been out here so long I sometimes forget myself.'

The stranger shuffled back to the campfire. He was a tall man of wide girth and wore a thick coat made of sackcloth. His hair flowed long and wild down the middle of his back. Sean noticed his feet were wrapped in rough cloth, fastened by string. His eyes glinted in the firelight.

'Okay, suit yourselves,' said the stranger. 'I'm not going to hurt ya. Not old Jake. If it's the house you're looking for, it's way over yonder,' he said, pointing into the distance. 'But you'll have a devil of a time finding it in this fog.'

Sean and Emily watched the stranger from the safety of the trees. He sat alone, stirring a pot over the campfire.

'Let's go,' said Sean

'I don't like this,' said Emily.

'He looks harmless enough to me.'

'Harmless? He's huge!'

'What are you two muttering about?' said Jake. 'I have some stew going spare if you foxes are hungry?'

Emily followed Sean's lead and edged closer to the

campfire. By the firelight, Sean noticed a ramshackle hut leaning against the trunk of a gnarled, old tree. It was made of corrugated iron and scraps of wood. Around its rafters, animal skins and tin cans dangled on strings while a collection of barrels and assorted junk lay beside it on the ground.

Jake handed them each a steaming tin can wrapped in sackcloth.

'Take a seat,' he said, pointing to a circle of logs near the fire.

'Thanks, it smells good,' said Sean, trying to be polite.

Jake continued to stir the pot and whistled a tune like he was in another world. Sean blew steam from his soup and took a sip. It tasted meaty.

'And what brings you cubs out into the woods on an evening like this?'

Sean and Emily exchanged glances, unsure what to say.

'We got lost,' said Sean.

'I'd figured that much out myself.'

Emily nudged Sean's arm and made him spill a puddle of soup on the ground.

'If I didn't know better, I'd say you two were treasure hunters. But where are your metal detectors and spades?'

'Have you seen a lot of them in the woods?' said Emily.

'Over the years. I think most of them have given up by now.'

Sean gestured towards Emily and urged her on.

'What were they looking for?' said Emily.

Jake stood and stretched his considerable frame. His silhouette was a fearful sight against the campfire.

'You tell *me,* young vixen. Why can't they leave old Jake in peace, eh?'

Emily spluttered on her soup.

'Present company accepted, of course.'

'We heard there was a legend,' said Sean.

'Ha, I knew it! I can smell 'em a mile away. I knew they were treasure hunters!'

Emily huffed and gave Sean a dirty look.

'But we only heard part of it,' said Sean, winking at Emily.
'What would you like to know, young cub?'
Sean took a deep breath and chose his words carefully.
'Is there really any treasure out here?'
Jake performed a little dance on the spot and shook his head in amusement.
'He ventures out into a misty woods, and he doesn't even know if there's any treasure?'
Jake continued to chuckle and returned to his pot.
'There's treasure everywhere in life, young cub. But most people are too blind to see it when they find it.'

****

Clavity's boots brushed the upper branches of a giant oak tree. He scanned the woods floor below, and his infrared visor showed a cold, empty scene. The Kimbleton guards struggled to make progress in the fog, and Clavity listened to their chatter on his earpiece. After about five minutes of flight, he noticed a tiny speck of warmth and moved in for a closer look. He nudged his hoverpack controls, and the yellow speck grew into several orange and red patches.
Clavity swooped down, but in his haste, he forgot to change his scanner settings. His right leg snagged against a branch, and he cartwheeled head over heels. His arm was pinned down by his side, which forced his wrist against the hoverpack's throttle. In response, it reduced power, and Clavity plummeted through the canopy. He bounced like a pinball against a tree and landed with his legs splayed on either side of a lower branch. He cried out in agony and toppled headfirst into a pile of leaves.
'Ah, Major. Good of you to drop by!' said a familiar voice. 'Were you missing me already?'
Clavity rolled over in the leaves and clutched his groin. Through his tears, he recognised a shiny bob of black hair walking towards him. She was dressed in a camouflaged outfit.

'I see you still haven't mastered your hoverpack?'

Clavity recognised her smile at once. It was Rusham, and by the look of it, she had succeeded in joining the commandos.

'What are you doing here?'

'Playing boy scouts mostly. By the way, you are now my prisoner. Don't move, or I'll have to shoot you.'

'What?'

'Sentry duty,' said Rusham. 'It was either that or skinning rabbits.

'Sorry?'

'Basic training, Major. We have to fend for ourselves and traipse around in the mud like animals.'

'Err, why?'

'To prove how tough we are. Don't you remember anything from your Army days?'

Clavity rolled into a crouched position and switched off his hoverpack.

'Stay right where you are, prisoner! State your name, rank, and mission.'

Clavity groaned and rose to his feet. A moment later, his left leg gave way. He sailed over Rusham's boot and landed heavily on the ground.

'Nice try, prisoner. Name, rank, and mission?' said Rusham, relishing the opportunity to throw her ex-boss around.

Clavity lay on the ground moaning as Rusham pressed her boot against his chest and locked his left arm in an Aikido grip.

'Clavity, Major. I'm on an undercover mission for the Founder.'

'Doing what?' said Rusham, twisting his wrist for added discomfort.

'Ahh! You're hurting me.'

'That's kind of the point, prisoner.'

'Alright, I'll tell you. *Provided* you take your boot out of my face.'

Rusham released his arm, drew her blaster, and took a step back.

'And what do we have here, Cadet Rusham?' said a male voice.

Clavity sat up and rubbed his sore wrist. He recognised Captain Ayres's smug grin at once.

'Just what I need,' he muttered.

'A surprise attack, sir,' said Rusham.

'Major Clavity, eh? Nice try, but you'll find my cadets are equal to any challenge. By the way, give my regards to your desk.'

Ayres laughed and hurried away to share the news.

'What are you really doing here?' said Rusham, putting her weapon back in its holster.

'Sean and Emily have gone missing from Kimbleton Hall, and Brawne thinks Krankhausen is behind it.'

Rusham frowned.

'I doubt it. They were probably bored to death cooped up in that stuffy, old house. Have you tried Sean's watch?'

Clavity gave a shrug.

'How do you mean?'

'Don't all standard-issue watches have a built-in tracking signal and communicator?' said Rusham. 'You *gave* him one, remember?'

Clavity gritted his teeth. How could he have forgotten?

'Yes, of course. But it's tricky getting a signal with all these trees and the mist. Anyway, I need to go.'

'Can we help?'

'I'll call you if they don't find him soon. It's politics. You know how things are?'

'Yeah. And Ayres will be telling everyone about your capture for months.'

Clavity winced. He switched his watch to search mode and waited for a satellite connection. A bright red circle lit up its display.

'Gotcha!'

'Yeah, funny stuff this *mist*,' said Rusham. 'Go get him,

Uncle Clavity.'

****

Spy-bot 12-59 left the Untold Sacrifice's cargo bay and floated across a grassy park surrounding the Foundation's HQ. It knew the site well from previous visits and made its way towards a large, white building. Concealed by light reflectors, 12-59 crossed a lawn and opened a fire door by remote control. It glided into a corridor and scanned for alarms. There was nothing unusual, and it continued its journey.

'Locating data libraries.'

'Continue your mission,' said 102, from the Untold Sacrifice.

12-59 discovered the majority of the Foundation's staff were busy repairing vehicles. It slipped through a series of electronically controlled doors and sped towards its target. Once inside the Foundation's data centre, 12-59 probed the main computer. It discovered Sean Yeager's files had been moved to a private storage device in Professor Quark's personal laboratory. 12-59 worked out the quickest route and glided down another spotless corridor. While it travelled, 12-59 calculated it would have access to all the Foundation's secrets within three Terran minutes. It floated around a corner and struck a wall of pure energy.

'Mobility malfunction! Mobility malfunction!'

12-59 hung suspended in mid-air. It tried to escape and found itself pinned by a powerful magnetic field. Its transmitter and sensors stopped working, and it was helpless. A peel of alarms echoed through the laboratory wing.

'What is it, Fullbright?' said Quark, interrupting his evening break.

'The Flytrap has caught an intruder, sir. It looks like some kind of machine.'

'Call out the guard! I'll meet you outside my office.'

Quark gulped down the last of his coffee and brought the

rest of his sandwich with him. By the time he reached his office, a crowd of guards had gathered outside and were arguing about tactics.

'What are your orders, sir?' said Edmondson, the head guard.

'To apprehend the intruder, of course.'

Edmondson looked bemused.

'I would, sir. But it's surrounded by an energy field.'

'Ah yes, I see your dilemma.'

Fullbright barged his way through a crowd of trigger-happy guards and commandos.

'It's an advanced machine, Professor. Its outer casing is reflecting every scanner we have.'

Quark turned to Edmondson.

'Deploy your most powerful plasma cannons. If it moves, disintegrate it.'

'Yes, sir,' said Edmondson, hurrying away.

Quark waved Fullbright into his office.

'Show me this *advanced* machine.'

Fullbright switched on a screen. They watched 12-59 shimmer in and out of focus like a giant, metallic egg covered in blue sparks.

'Now what do we do?' said Quark. 'If we lower our defences, who knows what that thing's capable of?'

'We could try communicating with it, sir.'

'And ask it to surrender? Yes, I'm sure if we ask nicely...'

****

Inside Laboratory-four, a defrosted spyder-bot stretched out its legs and checked its power cells. They were fully charged. Its outer shell had sustained only minor damage, and it wriggled its muscles. It found itself dripping with condensation inside a plastic cube. Hidden by a cloud of moisture, the spyder-bot set to work. It activated a laser and burned a circular hole in the bottom of the cube. Next, it cut through a glass case and a steel bench. When the smoke had cleared, the spyder-bot folded its limbs and dropped through the aperture. It landed on a floor panel and detected a hollow space beneath its feet. The spyder-bot sliced through a plastic tile and dropped into a cavity. Sensing alarm systems all around, it homed in on their signals.

After a short scuttle under the laboratory floor, the spyder-bot found a bundle of cables and cut into their plastic sheaths. It was so focused on its task it failed to detect the pitter-patter of an approaching prowler-bot. It burned its way through a live cable and shut down the laboratory wing's security system.

CHAPTER 12: CONFINED

Hughes took his time on the return to Kimbleton Hall and switched the quad bike's lights to full beam.

'Do you have any idea how much trouble you've caused?'

Sean and Emily clung to the back of his seat and remained silent.

'I don't get it. Why did you go out into the middle of the woods? You know it's forbidden?'

Sean and Emily did not reply because the quad bike's engine drowned out most of Hughes' words.

'Bird's Nest, this is Hughes. Come in, Bird's Nest.'

'Go ahead, Hughes, over.'

'I've found the runaways, sir.'

'Thank goodness! Are they in one piece?' said Brawne.

'Yes, sir. I found them huddled around a campfire.'

'Really? Bring them in for a debrief. Oh, and good work, Hughes.'

'Thank you, sir.'

Hughes felt a mixture of relief, anger, and astonishment. He had mysteriously received Sean and Emily's location on his phone. He had no idea where it came from, but it must have been someone using Foundation equipment. It also puzzled him how Sean and Emily had found their way to an abandoned campsite and lit a fire. He'd heard rumours of a tramp who once lived deep inside the woods. However, the woodsman's hut had been abandoned for years. Could Sean and Emily have chanced upon it and lit their own fire? They also claimed to have met someone called Jake and yet there was no trace of anyone at the campsite.

'Whatever,' he thought. 'At least they're safe.'

Hughes drove on and looked forward to his sandwich.

****

Edmondson's men set up two large plasma cannons in the corridor outside Quark's office. From shielded positions, they watched 12-59 hover and spin inside a blue haze. However, Professor Quark was a worried man.

'If it gets out, it could destroy the HQ and all our work.'

'Or steal our secrets?' said Fullbright.

They watched the group of trigger-happy guards.

'What would happen if they hit the Flytrap?'

Fullbright shook his head.

'The worst they can do is melt the field projectors and disable its electromagnets.'

Suddenly, the strip lights above them went out, and the corridor was plunged into darkness. The plasma field vanished, and 12-59 hovered lower. Edmondson's men fired a barrage of energy-bolts, and 12-59 span around deflecting them. The first pierced Quark's office door and whizzed past his head. It struck a screen behind him, which exploded. Several more struck the corridor's walls, and one hit the Flytrap's ceiling array. Unscathed, 12-59 hovered clear of the weakened magnetic field.

'Cease fire!' cried Quark, on his hands and knees.

12-59 floated down the corridor and scanned the area. Satisfied it was safe, it began to mind-probe everyone in the vicinity. The guards froze, and one by one, their eyes glazed over.

'What's happening?' said Quark.

Fullbright fell silent and stood like a mannequin. His eyes froze, and his mouth fell open. Quark felt a presence in his mind and drifted into a dream-like state.

'You will unlock your data files and tell me who created the Matteract device,' said a synthetic voice inside his mind.

'Never! Get out of my head!'

****

Sean and Emily climbed Kimbleton Hall's staircase in their bare feet with their ears still ringing. Everyone was angry about their expedition into the woods, especially Mrs Campbell. After a shower and a change of clothes, they had been questioned for almost an hour. Sean had admitted it was his fault, but Emily had been equally chastised.

'Do you think they'll really ground us for a month?' said Sean.

Emily sighed and continued her slow climb.

'Yep, you've done it now. If Brawne had his way, we'd be locked in the cells.'

Sorry.'

He resisted the urge to rub his shoulder. After a quick examination, the medic had covered his wound in iodine and plastic skin. He said it was only a small bite, but it still throbbed like crazy. Sean reached his bedroom door.

'Good night, Em.'

'Night,' said Emily, heading to her room.

Sean switched on the light and closed his door.

'And here's the drowned rat now,' said a familiar voice.

Sean found the cat curled up in the middle of his bed. It lay at the end of a trail of muddy footprints on a pale-yellow bed cover.

'Look what you've done! Mrs Campbell will have a fit.'

'Boohoo, I'm scared. I think you're the one in the doghouse this month, Einstein.'

Sean hurled a cushion, but the cat ducked sideways, and it flew over its head.

'Hey, play nice.'

'Call yourself a bodyguard?'

The cat sat upright in a regal pose.

'And who do you think found you? A flying clown?'

Sean frowned.

'Was it *you* who shot the dragonflies?'

'That's classified information. No comment,' said the cat, rubbing its nose with its paw. 'I *may* have followed your scent.

You stink, by the way.'

'Thanks,' said Sean, unsure whether to be grateful or annoyed.

'For saving you or giving you hygiene advice?'

****

Professor Quark strode past a huddle of motionless guards and made for his private laboratory. 12-59 floated along beside him and shone a beam of white light for his benefit. He stopped beside a heavy door and used a metal key to open a flap in the wall. It clicked open, and he turned a hydraulic release valve. It was hard work, and Quark was soon flushed.

'Stop!' commanded a voice further along the corridor.

12-59 turned and scanned a tall figure wearing an oversized sackcloth coat. Quark relaxed his grip on the valve and slumped against the wall.

'Identify yourself,' said 12-59, activating its mind-probe circuits.

'I am Cassius Olandis,' said the pale man, his eyes glinting. 'By order of Aenaid compliance code nine-zero-nine-zero-nine, I command you to obey me.'

The spy-bot hovered for a moment and consulted its memory banks.

'Compliance code accepted. Overriding compliance code.'

'Obey me!'

12-59 flashed and span around in the air, its circuits buzzing.

'Activating memory wipe.'

'Stop! I command you!' cried Olandis.

12-59 fell to the floor with a thud, and Quark woke with a start.

'Where am I?'

Olandis smiled.

'You are quite safe, Professor.'

In the shadows, a tiny spyder-bot limped forwards on six claw-tipped legs. It clattered towards Olandis and extended two poisonous spines near its mouth. Tensing its remaining legs, it sprang up at his exposed neck. In mid-flight, two arcing beams of light met and fried the spyder-bot to a crisp. A pair of silver figures appeared out of the gloom and lowered their weapons.

'What's going on?' said Quark.

****

Dr Vex wandered aimlessly around the bridge of the Untold Sacrifice. There was little to occupy his mind except thoughts of escape. Fearing for his life, he tried to focus on the mission.

'Why hasn't 12-59 reported its findings?'

102 appeared in female form, wearing the flight suit of a battleship commander.

'I have tried to contact 12-59, and it is not responding.'

'I'm not surprised. It's a heap of junk if you ask me.'

'Who asked you this question?' said 102.

Vex laughed, and the hologram scowled back.

'Why don't I go and look for it?'

'It is not necessary for you to look for 12-59.'

Vex scuffed his heels on the deck.

'What *are* we going to do then? Sit around here and wait? What if that heap of junk really has broken down?'

102 transformed itself into a giant land marauder clad in body armour. It extended itself to the ceiling and glared.

'If 12-59 has broken down, *I* will recover it.'

'And leave your ship unprotected?'

102 vanished without saying another word. Vex was now familiar with the sentient's erratic behaviour and used his free time to explore the storage deck. Most of the lockers were sealed, except for one. He opened it and discovered a black resin case secured by a simple lock. He hauled it out and carried it to the engine bay. He reasoned the energy fields there would shield him from 102's sensors. Vex positioned the case beside a power transformer and prised open its lock.

It contained a small, metal sphere covered in intricate grooves. The sphere was a dull grey colour and filled the palm of his hand.

Vex ran his fingers over it, and long-forgotten memories filled his mind. He pictured an Aenaix training session and felt the ridges of a similar object in his hand. His pulse raced. He returned the sphere to its case and wedged it behind the transformer. Vex hurried back to the bridge and waited. Would he be found out? And more importantly, would he be punished?

Several long minutes passed before 102 reappeared. It projected the body of an older man in the regalia of a general.

'Dr Vex, we need you to find 12-59,' it said in a stern voice.

'Where should I start?' said Vex, pretending to be interested.

102 put on a serious expression.

'We will be monitoring your every thought. Do not try to escape.'

Vex smiled.

'Actually, I think I need to stay here and plan our next move. You can go and recover your colleague.'

102 stared blankly.

'That is impossible, Dr Vex. I am unable to leave the Untold Sacrifice.'

Vex took a deep breath and smiled. At last, a weakness.

'I think we should focus our efforts on this Yeager boy, don't you? I'm sure 12-59 can look after itself?'

102's avatar quivered and faded. It was replaced by a projection of Deijan Klesus, who spoke in a serious tone.

'Dr Vex, this mission depends on your co-operation. The future of our entire race lies in your hands. We need you to recover all Aenaid life on Terra.'

Vex folded his arms.

'If I'm so important to this mission, remove the mind probe and let me complete my work unimpeded.'

'I'm sorry, we can't do that,' said Klesus.

'Why not?'

'If we remove your mind probe, it will damage your brain and kill you.'

'Then disable your receiver.'

The hologram faded and returned as a fleet admiral in full dress uniform.

'Dr Vex, you will obey our wishes, or we will be forced to end your fourth life.'

'And guarantee the failure of this mission? I don't think so.'

102 flashed through several avatar faces and became a blur of shapes and poses. Its transformations became quicker and more erratic.

'Error code 379. Error code 379. Re-boot! Re-boot!'

Vex seized his opportunity and ran to the engine bay.

'Ship, take me to 12-59's last known location.'

'Affirmative,' said the ship's flight computer.

Vex recovered the black resin case and sprinted to the cargo bay. The ship touched down and lowered its cargo ramp.

'We have reached 12-59's last known location,' said the flight computer. 'You will need your exosuit, Dr Vex.'

'Now you tell me,' said Vex, approaching a rack of exosuits and leafing through them.

After a considerable amount of effort and grumbling, Vex strode out into daylight and tasted fresh air for the first time in his fourth life.

****

The next morning, Sean was woken by a series of loud rattles and thumps. He rolled over in bed and tried to ignore them, but the disturbance continued. A vehicle pulled up outside his window, and footsteps crunched across the driveway. There was a brief respite, and Sean relaxed. However, the footsteps returned and were followed by a clatter of doors and a whining sound like a hydraulic lift. Sean groaned and climbed out of bed to confirm his fears. Sure enough, it was a delivery truck. He muttered to himself and changed into some fresh clothes. Sean knew from previous deliveries that the noise would continue for ages. And now he felt hungry, really hungry.

The delivery driver pushed a trolley of food into the guardhouse door for scanning. After he left, a tiny mouse poked its nose out of the rear of the truck. It sniffed the air before leaping from the truck's loading ramp and landing on the driveway. A second mouse appeared and followed it into a rose bed. The two rodents twitched at each other and ran to opposite ends of Kimbleton Hall.

Sean dressed and sighed as he remembered the muddy mess of his new trainers. In their place, he found a pair of brown shoes. He left his bedroom and nearly tripped over the cat.

'Still here?'

'I'm surprised you waited long enough to find out,' said the cat, yawning.

'Why are you yawning? You're a robot.'

'I'm copying you, sleepy-head.'

The cat sniffed for a moment and swivelled its ears from side to side.

'What's wrong?'

'I can smell a rat. And I need you to stay inside the house. Do you think you can manage that? Or should I draw you a diagram?'

'Fun-ny!' said Sean, watching the cat trot away.

He stretched his sore shoulder and wandered into the hallway. By the time he reached the landing, Emily had joined him.

'Taking your *delightful* cat for a walk?'

'Err, no. I couldn't sleep.'

'Me neither. I kept having this weird dream.'

They staggered down the main staircase together and

winced at their sore limbs.

'What did you dream about?' said Sean.

Emily screwed up her face.

'It was freaky. There was a white light glowing in the palm of my hand, and then it floated over my head.'

'Were there any voices?'

'Yeah, they sounded like monks chanting.'

'Were they saying *save us* over and over again?'

'How do you know?'

They reached the ground floor, and Sean turned to Emily.

'I keep having the same dream. I think they want us to find them.'

'But who are they?'

'I don't know. Sometimes they call my name, but I can never see their faces.'

****

Mrs Campbell was already hard at work. She ferried cases of food from the guardhouse to the pantry and directed Maya to do the same. The maid was slow to respond, and Mrs Campbell hurried her along. Sean and Emily sat at the dining room table and helped themselves to an apple and banana from the fruit bowl. After a few minutes, Mrs Campbell poked her head around the door. She looked flushed and annoyed.

'You'll have to make do for now. I'm busy.'

After a drawn-out breakfast of fruit, porridge, and toast, Mrs Campbell repeated her lecture from the previous evening. If Sean and Emily were in any doubt they were grounded, it was soon explained to them again in excruciating detail.

'And Mr Steele wants to see you in the library after breakfast.'

****

Darius Deveraux summoned his second-in-command and relaxed in his favourite swivel chair. Seventy-one appeared in the doorway.

'Our spy-bots have entered the grounds of Kimbleton Hall, master.'

'Excellent. Do we know Yeager's current location?'

'Yes, master. We receive regular transmissions from his implant.'

'And where is he now?'

'Sean Yeager is inside Kimbleton Hall, master.'

Deveraux nodded and rose to his feet.

'It's time we ended this fiasco. Order our androbots to attack. They are to seize Yeager and eliminate everyone else. I want Kimbleton Hall destroyed.'

'Yes, master. It will be done,' said Seventy-one, transmitting the orders.

****

Sean and Emily trudged into the library and were greeted by Mr Steele.

'Good Morning. Do you understand why you've been grounded?'

'As a punishment?' said Emily.

'Yes,' said Steele. 'Not alone did you put your lives at risk; you also failed to complete your studies.'

Sean scowled.

'But we found the well and a tunnel under the house!'

Steele sighed.

'Indeed you did, Sean. However, I didn't ask you to go on a field trip, now did I?'

Sean swallowed hard.

'And we found out more about the legend,' said Emily.

'From a woodsman?' said Steele.

'He was more like a tramp,' said Sean.

Steele rose from his chair and closed the door.

'What did he say?'
'He told us that people have been searching for the treasure for years,' said Emily.
Steele glanced at Sean and Emily before clearing his throat.
'And do you think you can find it?'
Sean and Emily fell silent.
'You're right. There *is* a legend about a long-lost treasure,' said Steele. 'And if you finish your homework, you'll discover an ancient site near the drovers' road.'
Sean looked quizzical.
'What's a drovers' road?'
Steele ignored his question and raised a hand.
'However, you are *not* to leave this house. I shall return to hear your history report after lunch. This time, make sure you finish it.'
Emily gave an edgy smile.
'And have you read the book I left for you?'
'It was more like a film than a book,' said Sean.
Steele removed his glasses.
'What did you make of it?'
'There was an ancient tribe of people and an explosion in the sky,' said Sean. 'Afterwards, it snowed for ages.'
'But what's the point in learning about pre-historic tribes?' said Emily.
Steele sat on the edge of his desk and smiled.
'Ah, the innocence of youth. There's an old saying that history tells us where we have come from *and* where we are going.'
Sean tried not to laugh, and Steele rocked his head in recognition.
'I can see you're not convinced, Sean. But you will find we are all pawns in the grand scheme of things.'
Steele opened the door.
'By the way, Mr Brawne wasn't joking about locking you up in the cells. I'd be careful if I were you.'
Sean and Emily returned to their discarded books.

'Here goes nothing,' said Sean.

****

Vex marched down a dark corridor and chuckled to himself. He half expected to find 12-59 lying in a pile of wires and scrap metal. He was so pleased to be free of the Untold Sacrifice he failed to notice the walls and ceiling melt around him.

'Good of you to pay me a visit,' said a voice.

Vex reached for his sidearm, forgetting he was unarmed.

'I believe we can help each other,' said the voice, moving closer. 'It's okay, no one can hear you in this space.'

Vex clutched the case tighter to his chest. He found himself in a white space without shape or form and considered using the case as a shield.

'Where am I?'

'I knew you would come eventually,' said a man with sparkling eyes. 'Open your mind, and everything will become clear to you.'

Vex stood open-mouthed and dropped the case on the floor.

'It already is. And you can save your mind tricks for someone else.'

Olandis gave a quizzical look.

'Who are you?'

CHAPTER 13: INTRUDERS

Mrs Campbell entered the library carrying a pair of muddy trousers.

'Hard at work, I see?'

Emily studied an old map while Sean read a yellowed sheet of parchment.

'Yes, Mum.'

Emily traced a finger along a brown line on her map.

'What do you think this is? It runs across the whole estate.'

Mrs Campbell moved closer and produced a small, metal object from her apron pocket.

'Sorry to interrupt. I found this in your trouser pocket, Sean.'

Sean's eyes widened.

'What is it?' said Mrs Campbell, holding the object aloft.

'Oh, it's just a torch.'

Mrs Campbell placed it on the table beside him and strode to the door.

'It's an unusual torch. I think you need some new batteries. Good luck, you two. See you at lunch.'

Sean slid the micro-cutter into his pocket.

'What is it *really*?' said Emily.

Sean smiled and touched his nose.

'Top secret. Anyway, where's this line of yours?'

Emily opened a modern ordnance survey map and laid it next to the older map. She found Kimbleton Hall and followed a green dotted line across the woods.

'Look, they both follow the same route. They go south of Kimbleton Hall and all the way through the trees. It must be the drovers' road!'

'Looks like a footpath to me. Have you checked the key?'

'And according to this book, a drovers' road was a cross-country path for herding sheep and cattle,' said Emily.

'But surely they'd all run away?'

Emily gave him a dirty look.

'And this old map shows a *tumulus* next to the drovers' road.'

'What's a tummy-less?'

'I'll find out,' said Emily, leafing through a history book.

After a few minutes, she sat upright and looked very pleased with herself.

'A tumulus is an ancient burial mound.'

Sean looked thoughtful.

'Perhaps that's where the treasure's buried?'

'Among a pile of bones?' said Emily, screwing up her face.

'What's this?' said Sean, pointing at a small, black shape near the tumulus.

'It's a house, and it's at the bottom of a small hill. It reminds me of a picture I've seen upstairs.'

'Upstairs? Well, you do need to read Mr Steele's book.'

'How can I? I don't have a copy.'

Sean grinned.

'You could always borrow mine?'

Emily's eyes glistened.

'And we could have a quick look at the picture before your mum gets back?'

Emily rolled her lower lip under her front teeth.

'You're devious; do you know that?'

'And?'

'And I think we have just enough time before lunch,' said Emily, grinning.

****

A brown mouse ran towards the main gate at Kimbleton Hall. It scampered under a miniature hedge and paused to sniff at the air. The mouse twitched its nose and hurried on its way. Under the shadow of the hedge, it scurried towards a gatehouse and followed music from a radio.

Guard Miller sat at the gatehouse control desk reading a

newspaper. He glanced at a row of security screens and checked everything was under control. It was. Now the delivery van had left, he longed for his lunch break and a chance to stretch his legs. Miller sipped a mouthful of coffee. The radio annoyed him by playing another corny old song, and he changed the channel. Miller tapped his fingers on the control desk and scanned the security screens again. Everything was much the same. He settled back in his chair and turned to the sports section.

The mouse scampered across a red brick path and around the gatehouse. It reached a worn step and sniffed at a tiny gap under a wooden door. It wriggled nose-first into the gatehouse and paused to twitch its nose. Miller rustled his newspaper, and the mouse darted along a skirting board towards a waste paper basket. It reached the leg of a desk and climbed a rough, plastered wall. At the summit, it skipped over a bundle of cables, dodged between two display screens, and appeared in the middle of Miller's control desk.

'Squeak! Squeak!'

Miller was startled. He lowered his newspaper and found a pair of bulbous, brown eyes staring up at him. A tiny mouse stood on its hind legs and twitched its nose.

'Hey, fella. Sorry, I don't have any food.'

The mouse flicked its whiskers, and its eyes drew his gaze like a pair of optical magnets. Miller began to feel woozy and imagined the mouse's eyes had filled the whole room. Images of parcels and a man's face ran through his mind. He tapped his earpiece.

'Mr Steele, please come to the main gate. You have a delivery.'

In his mind's eye, Miller saw the front gates opening and his friends coming in for a chat. He disabled the security sensors and opened the front gates before slumping on the control desk. The mouse twitched its nose and turned to watch the screens.

Two grey figures entered the gatehouse. One pulled Miller from his chair and leaned over him for a moment, studying his features. It removed his jacket, sat at the desk, and pretended to read. Its face slowly melted and reformed until it resembled the guard. Meanwhile, its colleague pulled Miller outside. It lay his body under a rhododendron bush and stood over him. Its eyes glowed red, and it waited for Seventy-one to reply.

Mr Steele huffed and puffed his way along Kimbleton Hall's driveway. He knew from experience that the guards would refuse to bring his delivery to the main house. It was a long walk, and Steele wondered what it could be. As Steele neared the gatehouse, he saw a guard reading a newspaper and grinned to himself.

'Brawne would not be pleased if he could see you now,' he thought.

Steele knocked at the gatehouse door and entered.

'I believe you have something for me?'

The guard lowered his newspaper and gave him a cold stare.

'Hello? I'm Mr Steele. You called me a few minutes ago?'

The guard said nothing and pointed at the control desk. Steele noticed a tiny mouse staring at him. He gave a half-hearted snigger and was about to admonish the guard for wasting his time, but instead he found himself captivated by the mouse's enormous brown eyes. Steele felt light-headed and fell back into the arms of a stranger.

The second androbot laid him on the floor and extended its fingertips. It cradled Steele's head between its hands and concentrated. As it did so, its features and body shape transformed. The androbot grew a sharp nose and withered skin. Its hair thinned and turned grey while its back and shoulders hunched a little. The androbot put on Steele's clothes and glasses and strode towards Kimbleton Hall.

****

Vex knew something was wrong as he rolled 12-59 along a darkened corridor with the toecap of his boot. The brilliant white walls had vanished, and he was left to reflect on the stranger's offer of help. Vex hummed to himself and pictured a faraway island to mask his thoughts. He imagined a beautiful oasis of trees surrounded by a crystal clear ocean. The spy-bot was lifeless and rumbled along like a barrel. An unbidden voice drowned out his daydream.

'Dr Vex, return to the ship at once.'

Vex used his armoured exosuit like a battering ram and walked straight through a fire door. He rolled 12-59 across a lawn and up the cargo ramp of the Untold Sacrifice. A shining figure stood waiting for him.

'Glad you could make it,' said Vex. 'Can we move before the Terrans wake up?'

His instincts told him to go in search of Sean Yeager.

'Agreed, Dr Vex,' said the hologram of a female commander, hovering in the cargo bay.

Vex was shocked by her appearance. Where the sentient's appearance had previously been radiant, it now projected the muddled features of several faces at once. The effect was ghastly.

'Why is 12-59 not responding?'

'You tell me. This tin can of yours is only fit for incineration.'

102 examined the motionless spy-bot.

'Dr Vex, what have you done to 12-59?'

Vex felt his body shiver.

'I was ordered to go and recover it while you re-booted. Remember?'

'Remember what, Dr Vex?' said 102 in a flat tone.

'My mission?'

102 changed its avatar to a freakish blend of a fleet officer and a land marauder, one of the fiercest Aenaid warriors.

'What mission?'

'To find Sean Yeager and any Aenaid life on this backward

planet,' said Vex, feeling tiny beads of sweat collect on his forehead.

'Affirmative, Dr Vex. You will locate Sean Yeager and bring him back to this ship.'

Vex sighed.

'Can you take me to Kimbleton Hall?'

The disfigured hologram stared at him.

'Where is Kimbleton Hall?'

****

Emily hurried Sean along the first-floor corridor.

'Hurry, before Mum finds out we're gone.'

Beyond Sean's bedroom, the corridor snaked around a corner and under a pair of wooden beams. It opened into a small lounge area, containing a rocking chair and a coffee table. Emily pointed at a wall between two leaded windows.

'Is that *it*?' said Sean.

Hanging from a metal runner was a frayed tapestry. In faded colours, it showed a track winding around a stone cottage and up a wooded hill. Trees overshadowed the track on either side, and behind the cottage was a grassy mound. The tapestry showed two figures herding sheep. One of them was pointing his stick at the mound.

'I'm pretty sure that's the drovers' road,' said Emily. 'And the cottage must be the building on our map.'

Sean smiled.

'But why is the shepherd pointing at the tummy-less?'

'Tume-u-lus,' said Emily.

'Whatever. You don't know, do you?'

'He must be guiding the sheep.'

'To an ancient burial site?'

Downstairs, the front door slammed, and heavy footsteps echoed across the hall. Moments later, the staircase creaked and groaned. Emily and Sean looked at each other.

'Now what?' said Emily.

'Hide?'

They tiptoed along the corridor and crept into Sean's room.

'Under the bed,' whispered Sean.

The footsteps grew louder and reached the first-floor landing. Sean and Emily had only just managed to squeeze under the bedstead when the bedroom door was flung open. From their hiding place, they watched a pair of shiny, brown shoes and olive-green turn-ups pace the room. It was uncomfortable on the floorboards, but they held their breath. Emily felt something brush against her legs and stifled a scream.

'What was *that*?' whispered Sean.

'Your cat.'

'What are *you* doing here?'

'Saving your skins,' said the cat softly. 'When I give you the signal, run for the stairs.'

'But why do we need to run from Steele?'

'It's not Steele. It's an androbot,' whispered the cat. 'Watch.'

Steele threw back the curtains. He hauled the dressing table to one side and flung open the cupboards. While he was busy taking the room apart, the cat crept out from under the bed. Sean gave Emily a nudge. They knelt and peered around the end of the mattress.

'What are you looking for, metal-head?' said the cat.

Steele span around and raised his hands to reveal weapons poking out from his wrists.

'You've had a few upgrades, I see?' said the cat, leaping onto an armchair.

The androbot followed the cat's movements like a hunter. It made a spiteful sneer and charged towards it.

'Now!' said the cat. 'Run!'

Sean sprinted to the door and pulled Emily along with him. As they crossed the room, a beam of bright red light shone from the cat's mouth and struck the androbot's face. It screamed, grabbed the armchair, and hurled it, cat and all, across the room. The androbot peeled a layer of melted plastic from its cheeks and glared at Emily. Sean flung open the door.

'Run!'

****

Brawne sat at his desk typing a report about Sean and Emily's disappearance. He was struggling to explain how they found their way into the woods.

'Workmen left a manhole cover loose in the downstairs cloakroom and…'

'Pah!' he muttered and deleted the words.

In mid-thought, Brawne was disturbed by the howls and barks of a dog. Through the bars of his office window, he noticed Braveheart on the driveway. It had its hackles raised and was barking furiously at something in the distance.

'Stupid dog. Can't you see I'm busy?'

At the end of the driveway, Brawne noticed a row of dark figures trudging towards the house. He clicked on his earpiece.

'Miller? What's going on? Miller? Gatehouse, are you receiving?'

There was no reply.

Soon there were dozens of figures swarming down the driveway. The nearest began to run towards the house at a tremendous speed.

'Holy cow!'

He ran to the control desk and typed in a security code. The machine blinked, and a green light changed to red. Alarms rang out across the building, and Brawne made an announcement over the speakers.

'Emergency lock-down. This is not a drill. Repeat; this is not a drill. We are under attack!'

The guardhouse became a blur of activity. Guards swarmed in and selected weapons of all shapes and sizes.

Within a few minutes, the weapon racks were almost empty.

'Secure the West Wing and get all the civilian staff into the safe room,' said Brawne.

'Yes, sir!' replied a group of eager guards.

Hughes was on his rest break and sprinted from his quarters to the main house. As he crossed the driveway, he saw metal shutters slide into place over all the doors and windows. The fountain stopped spraying water and split apart to reveal a plasma cannon. Around him, the gravel parted, and a row of sentinel turrets rose into position. Overhead, the chimneys of Kimbleton Hall fell away to release missile launchers and laser cannons. Hughes realised he had seconds to reach the guardhouse before he became a target for Kimbleton Hall's defences. He sprinted across the driveway and saw a crowd of dark figures stampede towards him. They reached the lawn, spread out, and started to fire their weapons. Several took to the air, as they had done in Yeatsford.

'Androbots!' he cried, pounding on the guardhouse door.

'Get in! Quick!' cried Brawne.

'They're everywhere!' said Hughes, stumbling inside.

Heavy shields thumped into place, and the pounding of plasma cannons began.

'How many hostiles are there?'

'Hundreds, maybe thousands,' said Hughes, panting. 'We'll need electro-bolts to stop them.'

Brawne grimaced.

'But we only have standard rounds?'

'Then we need help, sir. Where are Sean and Emily?'

Brawne shrugged.

'In the library?'

Hughes ran to the armoury and grabbed an assault rifle plus a handful of grenades. He reached the main corridor and found two guards standing ready.

'Roberts, Nolan, follow me!'

****

Sean and Emily ran downstairs as fast as they could. Before they could reach the mezzanine landing, an androbot crashed through a stained glass window high above them. It fell in a shower of broken glass and landed in the hallway. Another androbot flew over their heads and reached the upper-floor landing. Their escape routes were blocked.

'Baba-baba! Baba-baba!'

The androbot in the hallway was hit by a volley of small arms fire and crumpled on the floor.

'Down here!' cried Hughes, crossing the hallway pursued by two guards.

'Phoom! Phoom!'

The Steele androbot unleashed a pair of energy-bolts which sent the guards scampering for cover. Hughes returned fire and sent splinters of wood flying everywhere. While explosions echoed around the hall, Sean and Emily cowered on the stairs. The Steele androbot aimed its wrists directly at them.

'No!' cried Sean.

At the bottom of the stairs, the Greek statues exploded in a shower of plaster and dust. A pair of metal skeletons stepped down from the plinths and stomped across the hall. They turned and scanned the scene, their eyes glaring red. Emily screamed. The skeletons raised their weapons and fired over Sean and Emily's heads. On the landing, the androbots slumped where they stood. However, their armour absorbed most of the impact, and they returned fire from prone positions. Bolts of blue electricity struck the metal skeletons, making them spark and hiss. They staggered forwards and froze.

'Come on, you two!' said Hughes, throwing a pair of smoke grenades onto the stairs.

The hall began to fill with white smoke, and more androbots crashed in through the upper windows. Sean and Emily skipped down the last few stairs and ran across the hallway.

'We're trapped, sir. The West Wing is sealed off,' said a guard.

'Roberts, get them to the tunnel!' said Hughes. 'We'll cover you.'

Sean and Emily hurried down the main corridor.

'You've got to be kidding,' said Sean, noticing a metal blast door barring their way.

'It's okay, the cloakroom is just here,' said Emily, opening a side door.

Behind them, Hughes and his team retreated into the corridor, firing as they moved. An energy-bolt struck the wall beside them and ripped a hole in the stonework.

'Roberts, open the escape passage!' cried Hughes.

'Yes, sir.'

Roberts squeezed past Emily and threw the rug aside. He dragged the manhole cover across the floor by its handle and dumped it by the sink.

'Ready to go, sir.'

'Sean, Emily, get down there!' said Hughes. 'It's your only chance.'

'What about you?' said Sean.

'We'll take care of the hostiles and follow you.'

Emily hastened down the spiral steps pursued by Sean. At the bottom, the passageway was pitch black.

'Do you have a torch?' said Emily.

'No, we'll have to feel our way.'

They reached the first wooden door, and Sean pushed it open.

'Woomph!'

A blast of red light hit the ceiling a fraction above his head. Sean ducked and crawled back to Emily.

'Are you okay?'

'Just about. There's something dangerous down there.'

'An androbot?' said Emily.

Sean switched on his watch, which gave a faint glow. A loud explosion shook the ceiling above them, and a cloud of dust filled the room.

'Uh-oh,' said Sean.

'I'm scared!' said Emily.

'It's okay,' said Sean, putting his arm on her shoulder.

'But we've nowhere to go?'

'Until Hughes turns up.'

CHAPTER 14: SURROUNDED

Cuthbertson stormed into Quark's office, his face bright red.

'What on Earth is going on?'

Quark squinted over his computer screen, unsure where to begin. He winced at the charred walls and boarded up window. At least the power supply had been restored.

'Security around here is a joke,' said Cuthbertson. 'Someone's even had the nerve to steal my car! In broad daylight!'

Quark nodded sagely and leaned forward in his chair.

'Yes, Henry, someone *has* taken your car.'

'And what are *you* doing about it?' said Cuthbertson, putting his hands on his hips and puffing out his crimson cheeks.

'Repairing it. You *do* remember being locked in your car?'

Cuthbertson stared into space for a moment and smoothed his moustache.

'Ah, yes. It err…slipped my mind. Is everything else okay?'

Quark took a deep breath.

'Yes, Henry. Apart from the damage to the basement, the vehicle pool, my office, the security system, and the laboratories, everything is just peachy.'

'Excellent, keep up the good work,' said Cuthbertson, turning to leave.

Quark sat dumbfounded. Who was this person masquerading as the Brigadier? He phoned the head doctor.

'Dr Fettale? I'm concerned about Brigadier Cuthbertson's health. Would it be possible to arrange a check-up? You can? Excellent. Yes, tomorrow would be great. But keep it low-key. Yes, he does seem a bit muddled. You will? Thanks. Goodbye.'

A short while later, Fullbright burst into Quark's office and rattled the makeshift repairs.

'Have you come to finish the demolition?'

'Sorry, Professor, but you need to see this. There's an emergency at Kimbleton Hall.'

Quark selected live footage from Kimbleton Hall's security cameras, and the video wall flashed into life. It showed several views of a large, yellow-stone building surrounded by grass and trees. Quark and Fullbright gasped at what they saw. The grounds were swarming with dark-grey figures. Some fired weapons at the house, and others scaled its walls. They watched open-mouthed as turrets and laser cannons returned fire and occasionally hit an intruder.

'Crikey, it's an invasion!' said Fullbright.

'They'll be fine. Kimbleton Hall is built like a fortress.'

A moment later, the main entrance hall exploded in a cloud of dust. Quark watched aghast as grey figures filed in through the front door. He reached for his phone and speed-dialled.

'Captain Reynard? Are you back at the aerodrome? Good. Scramble Sigma Force! We have an emergency at Kimbleton Hall. Yes, Kimbleton Hall. I need your heavy troops over there right away. It's Darius Deveraux. And this time, he's brought an army.'

Quark listened to Reynard's calm response.

'And I'm coming with you. You can collect me outside HQ.'

Fullbright looked worried.

'Are you sure, Professor?'

'Some of my best scientists are over there. I'll be darned if I'll let Deveraux get his filthy hands on them,' said Quark, hurrying to the door. 'Call control and have them dispatch some agents in support,'

'Yes, sir,' said Fullbright. 'But how will they get there?'

'Glidebike, Hoverlifter, or taxis. Just get them there!'

****

Emily was startled by sounds of movement in the

passageway. Someone or something was following them.

'Did you hear that?'

'It's probably Hughes and the guards,' said Sean.

'But what if it's not?'

Sean uncovered his watch. It emitted a faint glow.

'Watch, alive. Send SOS,' he said hopefully.

Footsteps shuffled towards them.

'Is that the best you could think of?'

'Look, we can either wait here for the androbots, or make a run for it and get shot at.'

'Okay, let's run,' said Emily, nudging him forwards.

Sean and Emily crept around the door. Surprisingly, there was no laser fire. However, the next room was shrouded by impenetrable darkness. Sean stretched his arms out in front of him and stumbled towards the centre of the room. He bumped into a rough stone wall and crouched beside it.

'I've made it to the well,' said Sean. 'Follow my voice.'

Emily stifled a whimper and crawled across the floor.

'Keep talking.'

'Over here. I'm over here.'

Emily bumped into the wall and slumped beside him.

'Ouch!'

'So far, so good,' said Sean.

'Oh really?' said Emily, prodding him in the thigh. 'I've just bruised myself.'

'Shush!'

A creaking sound and a chattering of high-pitched voices echoed from behind the doorway.

'Androbots,' whispered Sean. 'We need to move. Take my hand, Em.'

Sean circled the well and headed into the void, hoping to find the second door. Instead, he bumped into a metal bollard, and a small red light blinked back at him.

'Careful, Em.'

Sean led Emily around the bollard and prayed it would not attack them. Moments later, they passed through the second door, and Sean heard his feet splash in a puddle.

'Not far now.'

'Phoom!'

An energy-bolt struck the tunnel wall, hurling soil and stones into the air. It was followed by a series of flashes and explosions as the bollard returned fire. Loud detonations echoed around the cellar and lit up the tunnel.

'Run, Em!'

Sean and Emily scurried down the tunnel until all they could hear were their own footsteps. Eventually, daylight broke the gloom, and they reached the woods. Sean ran outside and expected the blast door to slam shut behind them. Instead, there was silence.

'Why didn't it close?'

Emily shrugged.

'Who knows? Where to now?'

'We need to find somewhere safe.'

'No kidding? Such as?'

'What about that cottage in the tapestry?'

'Sure, and where's that?'

Sean gazed up at a luminous blue sky. It was a bright morning.

'You said the drovers' road runs south of Kimbleton Hall?'

'Ha, you *were* listening?'

'The sun rises in the east, and it's morning, which means we need to go this way,' said Sean, pointing into the woods.

****

Clavity patrolled the perimeter of the ruined cottage with his camouflage suit switched on. He worried about his equipment and checked his reflection in a field knife every couple of minutes. All he could see was an occasional glint of sunlight. As far as Clavity could tell, he was invisible. He packed away his tent and struck the campfire.

The woods were peaceful except for the occasional rustle of a passing animal. A gentle breeze ruffled the treetops and reminded Clavity of the seashore. Just as he began to relax, his watch vibrated and started to chime. He tried to silence it but found it was impossible while he was wearing gloves.

'Watch, alarm off!'

And still the watch chimed.

Clavity pulled off his glove. The watch flashed a repeating message: *SOS. Sean Yeager in danger. Request assistance.*

'Not *again*? Watch, locate Sean Yeager.'

The display showed a flashing red circle on a grid. Sean was two miles away near the commando training camp. Clavity called his ex-colleague.

'Rusham? It's Clavity. Sean's in trouble *again*. And this time, I do need your help. Yes, he's sent an SOS signal. Can you ask Captain Ayres to send out a search party? I'll forward Sean's tracker Id. Thanks. Over and out.'

He paced the ruins in a fluster.

'What are you doing, Sean?' he enquired of a nearby tree.

Clavity switched his communicator to Kimbleton Hall's frequency. It was strangely quiet. He toggled it backwards and forwards, searching for conversations.

****

The atmosphere aboard the Untold Sacrifice was tense. Vex tried in vain to convince AL102 that it knew the location of Kimbleton Hall. Worse, the sentient computer refused to believe it had ever been re-booted. It also denied any knowledge of sending a spy-bot to find Sean Yeager. In frustration, Vex demanded access to the Terrans' public information network, known as the internet.

'Look, it's right *here*. Kimbleton Hall and Kimbleton Woods. Can you scan the area, or would that be too much for your delicate processors?'

The sentient stared at him with the face of an elderly fleet admiral attached to the body of a female commander and the limbs of a heavy trooper.

'Affirmative. My scanners have detected a group of bio-mechanical life-forms attacking Kimbleton Hall.'

'Show me.'

A large screen lit up the front wall of the bridge. It showed an infrared view of a mansion house and its grounds. The scanner zoomed in to reveal a mass of blue figures moving towards the front of the building. Meanwhile, inside the West Wing, a small group of orange figures huddled together.

'Which one is Yeager?' said Vex.

'The Terrans are highlighted in orange. I have insufficient information to confirm the location of Sean Yeager.'

'Why not?'

'Vex Lauricus, it is *your* responsibility to find Sean Yeager.'

Vex shook his head.

'Any chance you could actually help?'

102's hologram hovered towards him.

'Dr Vex, it is *your* mission alone. Have you forgotten your life depends upon its success?'

Vex let out a resigned sigh.

'Same old threats,' he thought, feeling his heart flutter.

'Affirmative, Dr Vex,' said 102, without any hint of understanding.

'Since I'm putting my life on the line, I need weapons and armour.'

The hologram was silent for a moment.

'Negative, Vex Lauricus. You do not need weapons. You have been provided with an exosuit.'

'By Ze'us!' cried Vex. 'Do I have to use my bare hands to fight these savages?'

'No, you can wear gloves.'

****

Sean and Emily trampled through a carpet of fallen leaves. The air was fresh, and most of the trees were bare. They snaked through them at a brisk pace and ventured deep into the woods.

'How much further?' said Sean.

'I'm not sure, but the drovers' road runs all the way through the woods.'

'So it could be miles?'

'What do your feelings tell you?' said Emily.

'To hurry?'

Leaves rustled around them, and squirrels withdrew to a safe distance. Sean could feel eyes watching their every move.

'Something's following us. Come on.'

The trees thinned out, and they approached a clearing. There were a few saplings and fallen trees, but otherwise, the ground was clear. A gully ran from right to left and had steep, sloping sides.

'This is it,' said Emily. 'This *is* the drovers' road.'

'Are you sure? It's all wet and muddy.'

'What did you expect, tarmac? Let's go.'

****

Darius Deveraux's eyes glowed like red-hot coals.

'We have them, Seventy-one! Order our androbots to close in on Yeager.'

'Yes, master. Legion-one has broken into Kimbleton Hall, and Legion-two has surrounded the woods. Two of our spy-bots are tracking Yeager.'

'Excellent! Direct all our forces to his location. I want Yeager, and I want him alive.'

****

The drovers' road snaked through the woods. It led downhill and cut deeper into the earth. Sean and Emily zigzagged around fallen trees and crossed a small stream. After ten minutes of slipping and sliding, the track levelled out, although it was still very muddy.

'How much further?' said Sean.

'It should take us all the way to the burial mound.'

'And then what?'

'I don't know, but at least we'll be clear of the androbots.'

'Until help finds us.'

'Do you think they will?' said Emily, glancing at Sean's wrist.

Sean tapped his watch face and noticed a faint outline of numbers.

'I hope so.'

Sean remembered the micro-cutter in his pocket. He examined it in the daylight. It had a thin, blue line at one end but no buttons or switches.

'Your favourite toy?' said Emily.

Sean smiled and held it aloft.

'The cat told me it's a micro-cutter.'

Emily frowned.

'Which reminds me, how come your cat can talk?'

Sean laughed.

'It's not my cat. It's a Foundation robot.'

'Oh yeah? And it let you keep a weapon?'

'Finders keepers.'

Emily kept a wary eye on the object in his hand while Sean tried pressing it from every angle.

'Micro-cutter, on,' said Sean.

Nothing happened.

'Micro-cutter, activate.'

Again, there was no response.

Emily laughed.

'Did your cat tell you it was broken?'

Sean shook his head. He held the device at arm's length and took a deep breath.

'Micro-cutter, alive.'

A bright blue light sprang from its lower end and lengthened like a welding torch.

'Ouch!'

It singed a few hairs on Sean's wrist, and he let it drop. The micro-cutter fell onto a pile of leaves, and in next to no time, they were smouldering.

'Micro-cutter, off,' said Sean, stamping out the smoking

leaves.

'Just what we need to light a campfire,' said Emily.

'But not much use against an androbot,' said Sean retrieving the device.

****

The Untold Sacrifice touched down behind a small outbuilding inside the grounds of Kimbleton Hall. Vex sprinted from its landing ramp and ducked behind an ornamental wall. A battle still raged in front of the main house, and turrets fired at grey figures stalking the grounds. Vex came across a fallen soldier who had already begun to melt. He rolled the creature over and discovered a weapon in its hands. It was black with three barrels arranged in a triangle in front of a curved trigger guard. Vex knelt to pick it up. The weapon was a complex design for Terrans and surprisingly light. He guessed it fired plasma bolts.

'It'll do,' he muttered.

'What will do, Dr Vex? What are you carrying?' said 102.

'A piece of Terran equipment. Do you want me to find this Yeager or not?'

102 fell silent.

****

Sean and Emily followed the drovers' road downhill. It emerged from the gully and widened. Sean stood and turned his head from side to side.

'Can you hear them?'

'Who?'

'The voices. They're calling us.'

'Us?'

'Yes, they're calling our names.'

Emily looked startled.

'Crack!'

A twig snapped among the trees on their left.

'This way,' said Sean, wading through ferns and heading for cover.

Emily followed in his wake.

'What's over there?' she said, pointing at a pile of grey stones.

The outline of a collapsed arch rose in front of them. Around it lay the ruins of a stone building covered in moss and weeds.

'Looks like a good hiding place,' said Sean.

Sean and Emily picked their way around stone blocks and entered a fallen doorway. They took refuge behind the remains of a wall.

'Ouch!' said Sean, rubbing his temples.

'What's the matter?'

'It's the treasure. We're really close.'

'Great, the feelings are back. Did you bring a spade this time?'

'Very funny.'

Emily looked serious.

'Sean, we're being chased by killer robots. I don't think we have time for a treasure hunt.'

'Indeed you don't!' cried a male voice.

Sean and Emily ducked behind a wall and crept further into the ruins.

'Come out of there, or I'll make life *very* unpleasant for you!' cried the voice.

Emily peered over the wall. On the outskirts of the clearing, a line of dark grey figures approached in a semi-circle. They trampled through the ferns and trained weapons on the ruins.

'You need to see this, Sean.'

He stole a glance over the wall.

'Androbots!' he whispered.

A thin figure strode ahead of the approaching line and lifted his visor to reveal a pair of burning red eyes. He aimed his weapon directly at them.

'Your time is up!'

'Phoom!'

A surge of electricity struck Sean's body and made his legs give way. Emily caught him before his head struck a stone block. Sean lay in her arms and began to shake uncontrollably.

'Stop it! You're killing him!' cried Emily.

'Bring him to me!' cried Red-eyes.

Emily cradled Sean on her lap and noticed the stone bore a faded carving of the De Beaufort family crest. Sean opened his eyes. He was groggy and tried to sit up.

'We can't go out there; he'll shoot us,' whispered Emily.

'You have two minutes!' cried Red-eyes.

Meanwhile, androbots converged on the ruins from all directions.

'We have to do as he says,' whispered Sean. 'Help me up.'

CHAPTER 15: TRAP SPRUNG

Captain Ayres led the commando cadets towards Sean's tracking beacon. He studied his scanner and noticed a group of shapes moving near the target area. On infrared, he saw a mass of pale shadows and felt a shiver run down his spine.

'Right, squad, listen up! This is not a drill. We face a ruthless enemy who almost wiped out a support group at Yeatsford shopping centre. Use electro-bolts and aim for their chests. Above all, stay together.'

'Yes, sir!' said the cadets.

'Sergeant Briggs, take four cadets and cover our right flank. Rusham, take four cadets and cover our left. Everyone else with me.'

'Yes, sir!'

A voice spoke from the cover of trees, and a figure appeared.

'And I'm coming with you. I know exactly where they are.'

'Clavity, what are *you* doing here?' said Rusham.

****

Sean angled his heel and felt the ground flex beneath him. He scuffed a little soil to one side and realised they were standing on a wooden plank. He gave Emily a nudge, but she was too distracted to notice.

'Em, the floor. Look at the floor,' he whispered.

A blast struck a tree behind the androbots and set it alight. Another hit one of the androbots full in the back and propelled it across the ground. Red-eyes span around and gestured at a group of figures moving between the trees.

'Destroy them!'

The androbots took turns firing and advancing, and, soon, the clearing echoed with detonations.

'Commandos,' said Sean.

Emily gave a weak smile.

Meanwhile, Red-eyes turned and marched towards them. He was a few feet in front of the archway when a wall of shimmering light rose from the ground behind him. It spread in a circle and enclosed the ruins. Red-eyes paused for a moment.

'Yeager! You will come with me now!'

Sean stamped his foot again and felt the ground wobble. The plank felt soft and damp.

'Em, when I count to three, jump.'

'Stay exactly where you are!' said Red-eyes from the archway.

'One, two, three!'

Sean put his arm around Emily's waist, and together they jumped into the air like Maasai warriors.

'Crump!'

The planks bowed and cracked beneath them.

'Phoom!'

Red-eyes shot at the soil in front of their feet and inflicted more damage on the wooden floor.

'Again,' said Sean. 'One, two, three!'

'Crack!'

Sean and Emily landed underground on a pile of dirt and broken planks. Winded, they rolled sideways and peered around a gloomy cellar, which ran under the length of the ruins.

'Get back here!' cried Red-eyes.

Emily let out a shriek.

'What's the matter?' said Sean.

'My ankle,' she said, balancing on one foot. 'I think I've twisted it.'

Sean helped her to hobble across the cellar. At the far end, a flickering glow guided their way.

'I can hear the voices clearer than ever.'

'Where are they coming from?'

'Over there,' said Sean, heading towards the light.

'Phoom!'

A blaster bolt struck the ceiling, and an avalanche of soil and beams crashed into the cellar. Sean and Emily were knocked off their feet and covered by a cloud of dust. Fortunately, the roof above them remained intact.

'Are you okay, Em?'

'Just about,' she said, grimacing.

They brushed themselves down and staggered on. As they grew closer, Sean noticed a line of torches stretching away into the distance.

'Another tunnel?' said Emily.

'Come on! They're waiting for us.'

'Who are? The monks?'

'I don't know. I can't see their faces.'

'How do you know it's not a trap?'

'I just *know*,' said Sean.

A strong odour of kerosene hung in the air. The torches revealed an elaborate structure of wooden braces supporting the roof and walls of a tunnel.

'It's like a mine,' said Emily.

'Perhaps it *is* a gold mine?'

They rounded a long, sweeping bend and reached a pair of stone pillars lit on either side by torches. Above the pillars, a rectangular boulder bore a carving of the De Beaufort crest. In the flickering light, it seemed to fly like a bird of prey and beat its wings beneath a blazing sun. Between its talons, it carried a ring.

'Did you see it move?' said Sean.

'See what move? A mouldy, old stone?'

Sean ducked between the pillars and entered a cavern lined with smooth-faced rocks. It was lit by more blazing torches. Emily shuffled after him on her good leg.

'This is it!' said Sean.

'So where's the treasure?'

'Over here,' said Sean excitedly.

At the far end of the cavern, stood a plinth holding a solitary object shaped like a flattened stone. Sean approached and picked it up. It was a metal tablet, and its upper surface was covered by unusual symbols, which glowed when he touched them.

'Is that it?' said Emily.

'What did you expect? A treasure chest?'

There was a loud, rumbling noise to their left, followed by the sound of footsteps.

'Who's there?' said Emily.

'Would you believe people have searched for that tablet for thousands of years?' said a familiar voice.

A tall figure approached. He wore a long, sackcloth coat and wild hair, which brushed against the low ceiling. Sean and Emily huddled together.

'Jake?' said Emily.

The figure nodded and reached out a hand to claim the tablet.

'But what is it?' said Sean, offering it on a trembling hand.

'All in good time. May I?'

From the cavern entrance came a wheezing breath.

'No one move!'

Sean turned and saw two burning red eyes.

'Over here, Yeager! And bring the pebble!' said Red-eyes, pointing a blaster in his direction.

Jake stepped forwards and blocked Sean's path.

'Fool! Did you think your pathetic trap could ever stop me?' said Red-eyes, aiming at Jake's forehead.

'There's no way out, Deveraux.'

'You can't stop me, old man!'

'Whumph!'

A blaster bolt struck Deveraux in the back, and he slumped against a pillar.

'Phoom!'

Deveraux twisted around and returned fire. He hit an invisible object which fell against the wall. An armoured figure appeared, clutching his chest. Deveraux cackled and levered himself up into a standing position.

'Over here, boy! Or *he's* next.'

Sean froze. A second later, Deveraux fired again. A ball of

electricity raced through the air and stopped in front of Jake's torso. It struck an invisible barrier and fizzed away. A silver figure appeared and used its armour to deflect a series of further shots. It was joined by a second bodyguard who fired at Deveraux's hand.

'Ahhhh!' cried Deveraux, dropping his blaster.

Instead of surrendering, Deveraux's eyes glowed brighter and brighter. A blinding red light filled the room and began to pulse. Sean hid behind Jake and covered his eyes with his hands.

'No one can help you now, Yeager!' cried Deveraux.

When the light had faded, Sean peered around the folds of Jake's coat. Everyone except Deveraux stood spellbound and silent. Deveraux raised his palm to reveal two barrels extending from his wrist.

'Adieu, old man.'

An idea came to Sean in an instant, and he reached into his trouser pocket.

'Micro-cutter, alive,' he said and hurled it at Deveraux.

In mid-flight, the micro-cutter burst into life like a Catherine wheel. It span in the air and struck Deveraux's right wrist, slicing it clean through.

'Ahh!'

'Whumph!'

A second blaster bolt struck Deveraux's armour, and he fell to the ground. Major Clavity staggered into view, ready to fire again.

'Stop! Major! Stop!' cried Jake. 'We need him alive.'

Released from their trance, Jake's bodyguards stripped Deveraux of his weapons and body armour before tending to his wounds. They tied him up, pulled a thick hood over his head and dragged him in front of Jake.

'You were saying, Deveraux?'

Clavity limped through the cavern and holstered his blaster. His breastplate was dented and torn. Over his shoulders, he wore the battered remains of a hoverpack.

'Nice throw, Sean. Where on Earth did you find that?'

'Oh, I just stumbled across it.'

'In a cellar,' said Emily, grinning.

Jake pressed his hand against a slab of granite. The giant stone grated and turned to reveal a passageway lit by a string of LED bulbs. On the tunnel's floor, a platform hovered above a monorail.

'This way,' said Jake. 'I think you'll find my new toy most amusing.'

****

A deafening howl of engines drowned out the din of battle, and Dr Vex took cover behind the statue of a Greek goddess. A shadow loomed over Kimbleton Hall, and dust devils spiralled from the driveway.

'Crunch!'

A sentinel turret was crushed flat into the driveway. In its place, the blue-grey hull of an assault craft flickered into view. Ramps were lowered at its rear, and lines of heavily armed commandos stormed out. They ran across the gravel and blended into their surroundings, leaving only footprints and a cloud of dust. Their shadows spread out and launched tiny missiles at the remaining androbots.

'By Ze'us, what are these creatures?' whispered Vex, peering around the statue.

A sound of gunfire echoed from the house, and flashes of light reflected on the shattered glass of the entrance hall. Vex crept around the walls of Kimbleton Hall.

'In the name of Tantalus, how can I succeed in this madness?' he thought.

A familiar voice filled his mind.

'You have twelve Terran hours to complete your mission, Dr Vex, or you will cease.'

'Thanks for reminding me,' he muttered. 'I'm going inside the main house. Have you located Yeager yet?'

'Negative.'

'Great. Just keep me away from their shoot-out, will you?'

'Affirmative, Dr Vex. Your exosuit is fully operational.'

****

Quark sat impatiently in the hold of a Hoverlifter, eager to rescue his colleagues. Beside him sat three burly commandos. The pilot spoke over the intercom.

'Captain Reynard has issued the all-clear, and we're about to touch down. Best of luck, lads.'

There was a loud thump, and the rear of the Hoverlifter opened. The two nearest commandos wedged Quark between them and shepherded him down the loading ramp.

'What are you doing?' cried Quark, unused to being manhandled.

'This way, sir. I'm switching on your camouflage. Everything will look grey from now on.'

The commandos hurried Quark through what was left of Kimbleton Hall's main entrance. The front doorway lay in a pile of rubble, and androbots littered the hallway. Through a haze of smoke, Quark noticed shattered glass and fragments of wood and stone strewn everywhere. He shuddered at the repair costs.

'I'll have to hurry you, sir,' said a voice in his helmet. 'Reynard needs you to open the laboratory.'

They hurried down a corridor, and Quark removed his gloves. He pressed his right palm against a security pad and punched in a code.

'Whoosh!'

Blast doors slid apart to reveal a laboratory full of people. They broke into a spontaneous round of applause. Reynard and his men stood guard by the entrance.

'Thank you, Captain. Secure the rest of the house and the grounds,' said Quark.

'Yes, sir,' said Reynard, re-sealing the doors.

****

A surprise counter-attack by a second wave of androbots left Rusham and her squad outnumbered. Inexperienced cadets fired at the enemy but found them difficult to target among the trees.

'Captain Ayres, we could use some help over here!'

'No chance, Rusham; we have our hands full. Close ranks and dig in. Reynard is on his way with reinforcements.'

Blast waves struck the trees, and Rusham took cover. She backed against a tree trunk and aimed at an approaching androbot. Seconds later, Rusham was thrown sideways. Her head struck something unyielding, and she passed out. An explosion damaged the base of a nearby tree, which collapsed on top of her.

****

Quark hurried to a console at the centre of the safe room. He studied its read-outs and puffed out his cheeks in amazement.

'It's okay, Professor. I've activated the force fields. We'll be quite safe,' said a tall figure with long, scruffy hair.

Quark studied the stranger from head to toe. He wore rags for shoes and a dirty sheet of sackcloth as a coat. His eyes looked familiar.

'Do I know you?' said Quark.

The stranger removed his coat and a wig. There were gasps around the room as he stepped out of his footwear and revealed a pair of shiny, black shoes.

'Founder?'

'Call me Cassius. I need your help, Professor. We have much to do. Open your mind and hear me.'

Quark closed his eyes while a stream of instructions filled his mind. He woke with a start and crossed the room to speak to an assistant. Between them, they coaxed Sean to a chair inside a glass-walled, inner laboratory. Quark covered his shoulder and neck in alcohol gel while his assistant sterilised a set of surgical tools.

'I'm sorry, Sean, this will probably hurt. We don't have time for a proper anaesthetic.'

His assistant injected a numbing agent into Sean's skin, and Quark set to work.

'Ouch!' cried Sean.

'Nearly there,' said Quark. 'Here it is! Matthews, take this away for analysis.'

'Yes, sir.'

Quark dropped a soft, maggot-shaped object onto a small metal tray, and his assistant carried it to the other side of the laboratory. Meanwhile, Quark sterilised Sean's wound and sealed it with glue.

'How are you feeling?' said Quark.

'Sore. What is that thing?'

'A bio-transmitter. It appears Deveraux had you bugged. Is there no end to what that man will do?'

'Careful, he's just outside.'

'What?' said Quark, dropping the glue gun.

Olandis beckoned to him, and Quark approached a chair in the outer room. A pale-faced man wearing a bandage over his eyes sat tied to a chair. He wore dark grey overalls covered in dirt.

'It's okay; he's restrained,' said Olandis.

'But how do you know it's Deveraux? No one's seen him for years.'

'I need you to run a DNA test, Professor. I have a feeling there's more to this man than meets the eye.'

****

Captain Reynard ordered his troops to fly over the woods in formations of three. He was unsettled by reports from Captain Ayres and agreed to bring reinforcements. If the woods were still teeming with androbots, they were capable of wiping out a squad of cadets *and* Kimbleton Hall.

'This is Reynard. Ayres and his cadets need our help. Use short-range electro-bolts and watch out for any heat sources.

The hostiles are colder than normal, repeat *colder than normal.* And look for friendly transponder signals. We don't want to hit any cadets.'

'Yes, sir!' said his commandos in unison.

Reynard scanned the ground while skimming the treetops.

'I have a contact at two o'clock, sir,' said his wingman.

'How many bodies can you see?'

'At least six, sir. And they're under heavy fire.'

'Okay, listen up. We're going to join their left flank and wheel around to create some crossfire. Stay in formation and watch out for any friendly fire.'

'Yes, sir!'

Reynard led his troops in a wide glide path protected by his most trusted commandos. As they descended, energy-bolts speared past them from all sides.

'Come on!' cried Ayres. 'The hostiles have almost broken through.'

Reynard's heavy troops landed and ran through the trees, firing as they went.

****

Seventy-one closed its eyes and gathered information.

'Master, I have news.'

'Go ahead, Seventy-one. And I hope for your sake it's *good* news.'

For a moment, they stared at each other in silence.

'Legion-one has been destroyed.'

'What?' cried Deveraux, thumping his fist on the console.

'And Legion-two is in the woods, attacking the Foundation's troops.'

'How many androbots do we have left?'

His second-in-command twitched as more transmissions arrived.

'We have thirty androbots left, master. Correction, twenty-eight. Correction, twenty-seven.'

'No!' screamed Deveraux. 'And *where* is Yeager?'

'In the West Wing of Kimbleton Hall, master.'
'With my clone?'
Seventy-one turned to a console and activated its screen.
'We are receiving the clone's transmissions now, master.'
The screen showed a fuzzy grey picture, and speakers relayed a muffled sound of voices.
'Switch to infrared,' said Deveraux.
'This is the infrared view, master.'
'Hopeless! Activate its T-ray scanner.'
'It is done, master.'
The screen changed from grey to shades of green. It revealed the shadowy outlines of a room and a group of skeletons huddled nearby.
'Why isn't our clone moving?'
'Its muscles are overpowered by restraints and medication, master.'
Deveraux's eyes blazed red, and he kicked at the metal floor. He turned to Seventy-one.
'Activate the clone's detonation sequence.'
'It will be done, master.'

CHAPTER 16: INVITATION

Cassius Olandis paced a polished, white floor and waited for Professor Quark to report his findings. He studied the twitching figure of Darius Deveraux and tried to read his mind. However, he found a wall of energy pushing back against his thoughts. His bodyguards prowled on either side of the room and drew their sidearms.

There was a happy buzz around the safe room. Although the androbots had been defeated, the West Wing remained sealed, and its occupants mingled freely. Sean and Emily chatted to a laboratory assistant while Mrs Campbell busied herself making everyone cups of tea. Olandis frowned and stooped to examine Deveraux's neck.

'What's happening to him?'

'I wouldn't get too close, Founder,' said Quark. 'Heaven knows what he's capable of.'

Olandis watched the veins in Deveraux's neck throb. Deveraux's head twitched, and his body began to expand. His skin stretched like a hideous balloon and swelled around its bindings. In a few seconds, Deveraux grew to twice his size and continued to expand.

'Get back, everyone!' cried Quark.

And then Deveraux exploded. The force of the blast threw Olandis and Quark across the room and toppled Sean and Emily from their chairs. Screens shattered, and a fireball rose to the ceiling. People screamed and dived for cover.

Through an orange haze, the silhouette of an armoured figure flickered into view. It took a few steps and collapsed on the floor beside Deveraux's remains. The figure wore a pale blue battlesuit covered in electrical sparks. Its armour was badly damaged and hung in fragments. The battlesuit rose to its knees and opened its visor. As it did so, a blast of water from the ceiling quenched the fire and soaked his face. Meanwhile, staff hurried towards the flames with fire extinguishers. The figure struggled to his feet and stepped forwards.

'I am Dr Vex Lauricus from the Aenaid ship, Untold Sacrifice. Cassius Olandis, you and Sean Yeager will return with me at once.'

'I'm sorry, Vex Lauricus, but you know I can't allow that,' said Olandis, shaken but otherwise unhurt.

Vex raised his left arm and pointed a triple-barrelled weapon at Olandis' torso.

'I really must insist. You see, it's a matter of life and death.'

Olandis raised his right hand in a gesture of peace.

'Lower your weapon, and we can discuss terms.'

Vex smiled and watched Olandis roll a white sphere along the floor. It span between them and wobbled to a halt. At once, the centre of the room was filled with a cold, white light. The walls and ceiling shimmered and blurred until there was no outside world. Bystanders froze, transfixed and staring into space. Olandis led Vex to the centre of a circular plate embedded in the floor. After a time, they walked in silence, each aware of what had to be done. Vex stood in the middle of the embedded circular plate. He turned and saluted Olandis.

'An escape pod will take you to a personal transporter and freedom,' said Olandis. 'After that, you're on your own.'

'I'll take my chances.'

'I wish you luck and peace,' said Olandis.

'By Ze'us, I need them,' said Vex.

Olandis returned to the glowing orb and switched it off. The room became alive with colour and movement. Vex appeared to move in an instant from the edge of the room to a circle at its centre. He raised his right hand, and the onlookers gasped.

'Pax Olandis.'

'Pax Lauricus,' said Olandis, returning the gesture.

The lights went out, and there were groans around the room. When they flashed back into life, Vex had vanished.

'I don't understand. What happened?' said Quark.

Olandis touched him on the shoulder, and Quark shuddered.

'Our visitor was a friend, Professor. He shielded us from the worst of the explosion. Be grateful we are still alive.'

A quivering smile returned to Quark's face. Clavity helped Sean and Emily to their feet, and Mrs Campbell rushed over to comfort them.

'But surely Deveraux wouldn't blow himself up?'

'As ever, you are correct, Professor. It was a modified clone sent here to destroy us. We must find the real Deveraux at once.'

'Yes, of course. But how?'

'Use the tracking beacon you removed from Sean's neck. Boost its circuits, and use its signal to locate Deveraux's transmitter.'

'I'll see to it right away,' said Quark, gesturing to an assistant for help.

****

Safe aboard his submarine, Darius Deveraux groaned as wave upon wave of instructions filled his mind. He panted for breath and collapsed in his chair. In his head, three black eyes stared at him.

'Yes, great one. I will do as you command. I will not fail you this time.'

After a few minutes, he became aware of a figure standing next to him.

'Master, we have detected more signals from Sean Yeager,' said Seventy-one.

'It's the Foundation! Switch off all our transmitters. Take us into deep water and engage our stealth device.'

'Yes, master.'

Deveraux slumped forwards and passed out. His head lay on the map table, and blood trickled from his nose. It landed on a map and collected in a pool near Kimbleton Woods.

****

Professor Quark accepted a cup of hot sugary tea from Mrs Campbell. He sipped a few mouthfuls.

'Skyraptor-one, this is Quark. I'm sending you the coordinates of a target believed to be carrying Deveraux. Track the target and report back.'

'Will comply, over and out.'

Quark turned to Olandis for guidance. Olandis smiled, and his eyes glinted like silver discs.

'You *know* what we need to do, Professor. Excuse me.'

Olandis approached Major Clavity and led him to a quiet corner.

'How are you feeling?'

Clavity held his bruised ribs and grimaced as he walked.

'Not so great.'

'May I?'

Olandis caught Clavity's gaze and held his right hand over his ribs. Clavity winced for a moment and began to breathe more easily.

'I knew I could rely on you, Major. I will be eternally grateful.'

Clavity blushed.

'Did we really use them as bait?' he said, gesturing to Sean and Emily.

'Major, you are a soldier, are you not?'

Clavity nodded.

'And you know what must be done in times of war?'

'But they're so young?'

'And yet so gifted,' said Olandis, resting his hand on Clavity's shoulder. 'They were always protected, and soon Sean and Emily will be able to look after themselves.'

Clavity shook his head and glanced at Sean and Emily who were laughing and joking with Mrs Campbell.

'Do they know what's happening?'

'We are beyond the Rubicon, Major. They will find out

soon enough. Excuse me. Sean has a priceless object I need to secure.

****

Agent Stafford raced around cars on the road to Kimbleton Hall. Controlling a Glidebike was tricky, but the g-forces were exhilarating. He flew a few feet above the ground and swerved around the wreckage of the main gate followed by Agent Wright. Stafford raced down the driveway and realised they were already too late. The fighting was over, but there was debris everywhere.

Stafford coaxed the machine to a halt and ordered it to cut its engine. The scene was surprisingly peaceful. However, the devastated entrance hall and fountain were stark reminders of a fierce battle. Piles of armour, white puddles, and discarded weapons lay everywhere. Strangely, Kimbleton Hall's guards were nowhere to be seen.

'Stay alert, Agent Wright! This might not be over yet,' said Stafford, pulling out his blaster.

Wright scanned the buildings around him.

'Where is everyone?'

****

Captain Ayres was a worried man. He stalked the woods accompanied by three of Reynard's heavy troopers. The battle was over. Outflanked and outgunned, the androbots fell where they stood, unwilling or unable to surrender. The cadets had taken a dreadful toll, and only a few were unhurt. Fortunately, their armour had deflected most of the impacts, though several had not been so lucky.

'Rusham was around here somewhere. Check for transponders,' said Ayres.

Two heavy troopers took up defensive positions, while a third used his scanning equipment. The heavy troopers moved from tree to tree wary, of any surviving androbots.

'Captain, I'm picking up a faint signal over here.'

'Cover me.'

Ayres knelt beside a fallen tree and pulled a branch to one side. He found Rusham lying in her armoured combat suit, pinned down by the tree. She grinned at him with a bruised face.

'How's the training exercise going, Captain?'

'Take it easy, soldier. We'll get you out of here in one piece.'

'I'm not much use in two.'

Ayres pulled a flask from his field belt and poured a little water into her mouth. He called HQ on his earpiece.

'Where are the medics? We have casualties in need of urgent attention.'

'On their way, sir. They'll be with you in a few minutes.'

'Sergeant, set up a beacon,' said Ayres.

One of the troopers rustled through some nearby ferns and discovered a fallen hostile.

'Sir, you need to see this.'

Ayres trampled towards him and saw a pile of damaged armour and white mush where there had once been an androbot. Its visor was pierced by two tiny round holes.

'A laser blast?' said Ayres. 'Where did that come from?'

The soldier shook his head.

'It's not one of ours.'

****

Kimbleton Hall's library was unscathed. Olandis switched on a lamp and directed Sean to an armchair beside a round coffee table.

'I believe you have a valuable item of mine?'

Sean blushed and produced a dull, metal tablet from his pocket. He offered it to Olandis on the palm of his hand.

'Err, sorry…sir.'

'Call me Cassius. Place the tablet on the table, with the writing facing upwards.'

Sean did as he was told.

'Now, raise your hands above it and focus.'

'On what?' said Sean.

'Why, your father, of course.'

'But I don't remember him.'

'Then focus on his photograph.'

Sean closed his eyes and tried to picture the solitary photograph of his father he had seen at home. It showed him in uniform being congratulated by a colleague. Sean breathed slowly, and his heartbeat slowed. Tears welled up, and he felt a warm glow beneath his hands.

'Relax your mind,' said Olandis.

The tablet's inscription glowed, and it slowly unfurled into eight equal segments. Fronds of crystal grew from within and extended upwards like the stamens of an exotic glass flower. A brightness glistened through the crystal and cast beams of white light onto Sean's forehead.

'I can hear a voice,' he whispered.

'Ask him whatever you like.'

'He wants me to help him.'

'Ask your father where he is.'

'He's showing me pictures. I can see a jungle, stone ruins, and colourful birds.'

'He's alive and well,' said Olandis stretching out his hand and commanding the tablet to close.

'Please don't go!' cried Sean, slumping back in his chair.

'Now rest,' said Olandis calmly. 'Open your mind, and remember all you have seen.'

The crystal fronds contracted and slid back into the tablet. Its surface closed and sealed over, leaving only the glowing inscription, which slowly faded to black. Olandis tucked the tablet into his jacket pocket and placed a silver necklace on the table. It was a pendant shaped like a crescent moon.

'Hear me, Sean. This is for your mother when her birthday comes around. Be strong and look after Emily. You have much in common.'

Olandis rose and left Sean asleep in the chair. He opened a

doorway in the library wall and descended a flight of steps to an inner corridor. Behind him, the library wall scraped and slammed shut.

****

Mrs Yeager fidgeted in the back of her blacked-out limousine. The Foundation had again supplied a standard-issue, bullet-proof car. She had tried to demand a less obvious colour, but this time her request had been refused. After all the hanging around and waiting on Aunt Helena, she had given in.

After a few days, Mrs Yeager had realised Aunt Helena was not in fact dying. The care home staff had been very friendly and put her up in the visitor's room. Unfortunately, no one was willing to explain Aunt Helena's true condition, which was a combination of a mild cold, old age, and loneliness.

'Can I speak to Sean, please?' she said as they pulled away.

'Of course, I'll try the Hall,' said Agent Zabaroni.

A few minutes later, he clicked off his earpiece.

'I'm sorry, Mrs Yeager, there's a technical fault.'

'Again? That's the second day in a row!'

'I'll call HQ for an update.'

Zabaroni muttered quietly for a few minutes.

'Yes, will do.'

'And?' said Mrs Yeager.

'Sean's fine. But you'll need to stay at Foundation HQ for a couple of days.'

Mrs Yeager felt a familiar sense of unease.

'Why? I thought we were already living in a safe house?'

Zabaroni waited for her to continue. Instead, there was silence.

'I'm waiting for an explanation.'

'Apparently, there's been a small kitchen fire, and they need time to clean up the house.'

'And where is Sean now?'

'At Foundation HQ.'

'What a surprise! I would never have guessed.'

'I'm not sure what you mean, signora' said Zabaroni calmly.

'I bet you don't.'

****

New arrivals crowded into the grounds of Kimbleton Hall. A row of white vans filled the driveway, and it fell to Stafford to marshal them. He rolled up his sleeves and took on the role of traffic cop with surprising zeal.

'You're blocking the driveway. I need you to move your vehicle right now!' said Stafford to a clean-up squad.

A series of Hoverlifters ferried casualties from the rear lawn under the supervision of Captain Reynard. Professor Quark joined him on the terrace.

'How's it going?'

'Slowly. We need more transporters,' said Reynard.

'Call for ambulances if you need to.'

'Is that wise, sir?'

'For minor casualties only,' cried Quark, struggling to be heard over the roar of a departing Hoverlifter. 'Tell them we were shooting a film.'

Reynard nodded and relayed the orders.

****

Sean, Emily, and Mrs Campbell were driven away in a black car. Emily and her mother glanced back at Kimbleton Hall with sad faces.

'I hope it won't be too long,' said Mrs Campbell. 'But the house is in a dreadful state.'

Their driver eyed them in the rearview mirror and spoke in a chirpy voice.

'You'll be back soon enough. Two weeks at the most, I reckon. Kimbleton Hall is built like a fortress.'

'So I hear,' said Mrs Campbell.

Their drive was long and uneventful. The constant motion made Mrs Campbell sleepy. She slumped to one side and let out a loud snore. Emily tapped Sean on the arm.

'What's the matter?'

'Shh,' whispered Emily. 'She's asleep. Wasn't that crystal amazing?'

'The what?'

'The crystal you found in the cavern?'

'Yeah, I guess,' said Sean, bemused. 'When did you see it?'

'Before we left. In the study.'

Sean let out a yawn.

'It made me fall asleep.'

'But did you see anything?'

Sean glanced at the driver and whispered.

'Yeah. There was a jungle full of birds, some ruins, and it was like Dad was talking to me. Well, I *think* it was Dad.'

'Snap,' said Emily.

'You spoke to your dad as well?'

'Yes.'

Sean sat upright.

'Crumbs, where is he?'

'I don't know,' said Emily, sadly. 'He wouldn't tell me.'

'Or perhaps he doesn't know?'

Emily gave a shrug.

'At least he's still alive?' said Sean.

'True. Now all I have to do is find him.'

CHAPTER 17: MESSAGE

Deijan Klesus felt confused and concerned in equal measure. He scanned a report from Sentient AL102. It told him the clone of Dr Vex Lauricus had failed and been terminated.

'Alviqua, how does 102 intend to complete its mission?' said Klesus.

There was a long pause, followed by the sound of static.

'I am unable to contact Sentient AL102 at this time, Deijan.'

'Why not?'

'I have insufficient information to answer your question.'

'Keep trying; I want to know what happened on Terra Prime.'

'Affirmative, Deijan.'

Klesus shut down his neural connection and strolled to his personal computer. Sarfelt followed him and nudged her spiky armour against his legs as a reminder about their daily walk.

'Not now, Sarfelt. I'm busy,' said Klesus pushing her away.

He opened his private inbox and looked for messages from his friends and colleagues. His inbox was almost empty. There was one unread message, from a name he did not recognise. It read: *Klesus, bring knowledge to Edinnu. We have swimmers. Beware of the serpents clothed in light. Pax Olandis.*

Klesus realised it was a coded message. Although he did not recognise the sender's name, he felt a vague memory stir in the depths of his mind.

'Serpents clothed in light,' he whispered. 'Edinnu?'

Klesus accessed the Fleet's computer system and looked for camera views of spacecraft at anchor. There were three - a transporter, a shuttle, and an assault ship. Intrigued, he searched the database for Edinnu.

'Edinnu: a mythical garden of delights. Also known to Terrans as Eden.'

He logged off the system and returned to his living quarters for a snack. Sarfelt followed in his footsteps.

'Alviqua, how many ships do we have in port?'

Alviqua projected a full-size image of a radiant fleet administrator.

'Deijan, all our craft are currently deployed on missions. There are no ships in port.'

'Thank you,' said Klesus, returning to the kitchen.

'Will that be all?'

'For now, yes. Sarfelt, catch!' he said, throwing a piece of simulated meat protein over the creature's head.

Sarfelt rose on her hind legs and snatched the morsel in mid-air. She devoured it in a single bite and looked around for more, her eyes solemn and expectant.

'I know how you feel, old friend,' whispered Klesus. 'I know exactly how you feel.'

Klesus shook his head ruefully.

'Serpents clothed in light,' he whispered. 'I wonder?'

Sarfelt stared at him and dribbled on the floor.

'Shall we see what else we can find?'

The End.

(*of the second adventure*)

Read on for an excerpt from:

Sean Yeager Claws of Time

Thank you *for reading this story. We hope you have enjoyed it. If you have, please tell your friends and family.* **Please post a review on Amazon, Goodreads or a similar site. They really help other readers to discover Sean Yeager and his adventures.**

Sean Yeager *continues his adventures in 'Claws of Time'. Our sources tell us the Founder's past begins to catch up with him when Darius Deveraux and the Vuloz flex their might. Meanwhile, Sean and Emily are drawn into an unexpected series of scrapes when they search for clues about their fathers. Of course, if you ask us, we'll deny all knowledge of everything. What was your name again?*

For more information *about Sean Yeager's world visit the website at:*

www.SeanYeager.com

Titles in sequence:

Sean Yeager and the DNA Thief

Sean Yeager Hunters Hunted

Sean Yeager Claws of Time

Sean Yeager Mortal Thread

Read on for an excerpt from:

Sean Yeager Claws of Time

CLAWS OF TIME INTRODUCTION

Sean and Emily return to a refurbished Kimbleton Hall. Safe, but bored, they continue to search for the truth about their missing fathers. Meanwhile, satellites crash around the world, and a letter arrives demanding their immediate return to school. Their arch enemy, Darius Deveraux, has vanished in the wake of a mysterious skyscraper fire. After a plea to rescue Major Clavity, Sean and Emily must decide who they can trust. Hold onto your seats, it's going to be a most eventful journey.

CLAWS OF TIME : PIECES

Sean woke to the chill of early morning, troubled by a vivid dream. He remembered discovering a crystal among the ruins of a stone temple and winced at the thought of a giant snake he found lying in wait. He had tried to scare the creature away with a sword, but it had followed him everywhere. It had lurked in the shadows, always one step out of reach and ready to strike.

'Where's Emily?' he thought, rubbing his eyes.

It was half-past five, and the sun had yet to begin its daily voyage across the sky. Sean put on some clothes and cursed the central heating. He shivered in the corridor and knocked at Emily's door.

'Who is it?' said a distant voice.

'It's me.'

'One minute, Smee,' said Emily, rattling some furniture.

While he waited, Sean remembered the tracking device in Emily's shoe.

'Watch alive,' he said. 'Scanner on.'

'Scanner mode on,' said the lady of the watch. 'What do you wish to scan?'

'Scan for bugs,' said Sean.

'Please clarify your request,' said the watch, and flashed up a menu of options: a) insects, b) illnesses, c) surveillance devices, d) software faults, or e) alien life forms.

'Scan for surveillance devices,' said Sean, though he was tempted to choose the last option.

Emily appeared at the door wearing a thick dressing gown. She eyed him up and down.

'Morning, scruffy. What are you doing up so early? Lost your comb?'

Sean made a feeble attempt to smooth down his hair.

'That's *so* much better,' said Emily. 'Are you coming in?'

Sean walked to the centre of her room, his eyes glued to

his watch.

'What's the matter?' said Emily.

'Shush.'

'Now you're really freaking me out.'

Sean raised a finger to his lips and approached an oak cabinet. He opened a drawer and triumphantly collected a small, metal disc.

'Aha!'

Emily gave a shrug.

'You told me to look after it, remember?'

Sean grinned and tapped his wrist.

'And it shows up as clear as day on my scanner.'

'But you already know what it is?' said Emily in a haughty tone.

'Yes, but I have a plan,' said Sean. 'And it's genius.'

Emily sat at her dressing table and began to run a silver brush through her straw-blonde hair.

'If I remember correctly, the last time you had a moment of genius, we ended up lost in a forest surrounded by androbots?'

Sean cringed.

'Err, yeah. But listen, I think I know where they keep the crystal.'

Emily turned to face him, her eyes shining.

'The memory crystal?'

'If that's what it is,' said Sean.

'And what do you think it is?'

'I'm not sure, but the Foundation told me Dad's still alive. And perhaps we can use the crystal to find him?'

'Do you think it'll work?' said Emily.

'It's worth a try,' said Sean.

'So, boy genius, how do we find it?'

Sean cleared his throat.

'The cat told me that every night it patrols a restricted area somewhere in this house.'

'Your cat?'

Sean glared.

'Sorry,' said Emily.

'Anyway, that disgusting robot keeps bragging about how it can go anywhere it likes.'

'And?'

'And if we follow it, I think we can find the restricted area,' said Sean.

Unimpressed, Emily continued to brush her hair.

'Where they keep all their *secrets*?'

'Like the crystal?'

'And who knows what else?'

Sean checked his watch and noticed two flashing blips. He took off a trainer and held it up to his wrist. At once the watch flashed a code number in red.

'Thought so,' he said.

'Thought what?'

'They're bugging me as well.'

'Lucky you,' said Emily, setting down her brush. 'So, tell me about this restricted area of yours.'

Sean grinned.

'I've seen it. Well, part of it. There's a secret passage behind the library wall. Hughes showed me when I first came here.'

'And what if Hughes or Brawne catch us?'

'Who cares? What's the worst they could do?'

'Throw us in the cells?' said Emily, with a pained expression.

'Perhaps?'

Sean eyed Emily for a moment, willing her to agree.

'Do you have any chewing gum?' he said.

Emily frowned.

'What's that got to do with anything?'

Sean grinned.

'I need it to stick your bug onto the cat.'

Emily smiled.

'Won't it hurt the cat?'

Sean shook his head.

'I doubt it.'

'Shame,' said Emily. 'But surely it'll detect the bug?'

Sean gave a broad smile.

'Not where I'm going to stick it.'

Emily gave a wary expression.

'Or we could just sit around here and wait for school to start?'

Emily's eyes lit up.

'Oh, come on!' said Sean.

'But I *like* school. And I miss my friends,' said Emily.

Sean put his trainer back on.

'And do you really think they'll let us go back to our old schools? Deveraux *is* still out there, you know?'

'They might,' said Emily.

Sean raised his eyes to the ceiling.

'But Deveraux has sleepers *everywhere*.'

Emily gave a sympathetic half-smile.

'And no one's seen him for over a year.'

'So what? He's hardly likely to knock on the Founder's front door, is he?'

Sean's stomach gave a loud gurgle.

'I suppose it's too early for breakfast?'

'I expect Mum will be up,' said Emily, ushering him to the door.

'And don't say a word to anyone,' said Sean.

'Not even your bug?' said Emily, grinning.

Sean stared at the disc in his hand.

'Go on, out! You can study it in your own room. I'm going back to bed.'

Emily closed the door behind him with a sudden draught.

'I wonder?' mused Sean, eyeing the disc.

****

Brigadier Cuthbertson closed a meeting room door behind him. He dialled up a video call and took a seat. There was a click, and soon the heads of Cassius Olandis and Professor Quark hovered above the desk in front of him.

'Good Morning, Founder. I've sent you my report on the Adastra Tower mission. Are there any aspects you would like me to investigate further?'

'Good morning, Henry. We know Von Krankhausen owns the Adastra Tower, can your agents locate his other properties?'

'Yes, sir; right away,' said Cuthbertson, scribbling a note.

'This is only the beginning, gentlemen. If Deveraux can hide a troop of androbots in the centre of London, how many more does he have at his disposal?'

'And they have developed a more advanced model since their last attack,' said Quark.

Cuthbertson shuffled uneasily in his chair.

'What leads you to that conclusion, Professor?'

Quark took a sip of coffee before answering.

'My team has studied the mission data. Androbots are human beings re-engineered from the inside out. However, these models are faster, stronger and more difficult to detect than any we've encountered before.'

'But they're still only Deveraux's drones?' said Cuthbertson.

Quark took off his glasses and began to clean them.

'Regrettably not, Brigadier. They appear to be connected to their equipment. We recovered one of their flying craft, and it was sentient.'

'Meaning?' said Cuthbertson.

'Meaning, that the craft tried to attack us when we examined it. In fact, we had to dispose of it before it caused serious damage to our laboratory.'

'And what about its pilot?' said Cuthbertson.

Quark replied in a deadpan voice.

'It melted like a choc ice under a blowtorch. Just like their predecessors, these androbots have a built-in self-destruct mechanism.'

Olandis raised a hand to interrupt.

'In which case, we need to capture one alive. We must learn how to defeat them.'

'In which case, we need to set a trap,' said Cuthbertson. 'I'll draw up some plans, and we can discuss them later this week.'

'Excellent idea, Henry; please make the arrangements,' said Olandis.

'Will do, sir. And one last thing, our agents discovered an unusual object in the wreckage of the Adastra Tower. Apparently, it lit up their scanners like a Christmas tree.'

Cuthbertson displayed a small, charred disc to the camera.

Olandis scowled, and his face grew pale.

'Where did they find this, Henry?'

'Among the cinders of the fifty-second floor, sir.'

Olandis fixed him with an icy stare.

'Send it to me immediately, under armed guard.'

Before Cuthbertson could reply, the video link clicked, and the holographic heads vanished.

Quark sat facing Olandis in a private room overlooking an expanse of parkland and trees.

'Are you okay, sir?'

Olandis shook his head.

'We have to stop them.'

'Who? Deveraux?'

'Another time, Professor; it's a long story…'

Quark followed his superior out of the room.

'What is it, sir?'

Olandis stared into the distance.

'My worst nightmare, Professor. Excuse me, I have much to attend to.'

Olandis hurried away to his quarters, leaving Quark to reflect on his words. After several seconds of deliberation, Quark went in search of a fresh cup of coffee accompanied by a spot of lunch. He decided to call Brigadier Cuthbertson.

****

Sean put on his dressing gown and a pair of thick, woollen

socks. It was late at night, and the cat had already visited his room on its patrol. He left his trainers under the bed and tiptoed along the hallway to Emily's room. As agreed, Sean knocked twice, three times, then twice more.

'What took you so long?' said Emily.

'Are you ready?'

'Of course,' said Emily, grinning.

They crept down the hallway and took the servant's staircase at the back of Kimbleton Hall.

'What did you find out about my bug?' said Emily.

Sean whispered in her ear.

'It is a tracking beacon, but it doesn't have a microphone.'

'Then why are you whispering? We're not going to get caught, are we?'

'Well, we're not wearing our shoes, but they *will* catch us.'

Emily caught him by the arm.

'What do you mean?'

'Come on, we need to get to the library before the cat,' said Sean, checking his watch.

Emily stood her ground and squeezed his arm tighter.

'Not until you answer my question.'

Sean groaned and shook his arm free.

'I stuck your bug onto the cat this afternoon.'

'And?'

'And we only have a few minutes until they think you're in the restricted area.'

'You set me up?' said Emily.

Sean felt a sharp jab between his ribs and stifled a yelp.

'Do you want to see what's in there, or not?'

'I might as well since I'm going to get busted anyway,' said Emily.

Sean led the way across an empty corridor and into the dining room. It was eerily quiet, with only the faint glow of an outside lamp to ease the darkness.

'Hurry, the cat is in the hallway,' whispered Sean.

They entered a narrow room, lined on three sides by walls of books. On the fourth side, a pair of computers sat on an antique desk in front of a curtained window.

'Over here!' whispered Sean.

Emily squeezed behind the desk, while Sean switched on the computers and their screens. He left them to boot up and nestled beside Emily and a pair of heavy, velvet curtains.

'Now what?'

'Now we wait,' said Sean, checking his watch.

'When did you bug the cat?'

'While it was charging,' said Sean, peering under the desk.

The cat swaggered like a lion into the library and flicked its head casually from side to side. It turned to face the computers and raised its nose to sniff the air. Sean held his breath and felt a blood vessel throb in his neck. After what seemed like an age, the cat pricked up its ears and ambled across the marble floor. At the far end of the library, it stopped in front of a large bookcase and sat in the gloom. There was a loud rumble and a sound of scraping. A short while later, the scraping and rumbling returned, and the cat had vanished.

'Neat trick,' said Sean.

'What happened?' said Emily.

'The cat's gone.'

'You don't say?'

Sean rose from his hiding place and broke into a run. He reached the far end of the library and tried to stop. To his alarm, he discovered his socks had other ideas.

'Oomph!'

Sean slid across the polished floor and fell flat on his back. His torch clattered across the marble floor. Sean rolled onto his side and rubbed his sore behind.

'Soft landing?' said Emily, offering a hand.

'Very funny.'

'Can we turn the lights on?' said Emily.

'Sure, and why don't we phone Hughes as well? Just to make sure he knows we're here?'

Emily surveyed the room.

'Aren't their cameras watching us already?'

'And motion detectors, pressure pads, heat sensors, microphones, and laser beams,' said Sean, retrieving his torch.

'Huh?'

'But none of them are switched on.'

'How do you know?'

Sean smiled.

'Mum insisted. She hates being spied on. Shall we?'

Sean and Emily examined the bookcase, which was packed from floor to ceiling with books of all shapes and sizes. It was interrupted only by the rail of a stepladder, which ran the length of the wall. It all seemed much as Sean remembered from his long hours of pretending to do his homework.

'The cat was about here,' said Emily, pointing at the floor.

Sean stamped on the tiles. They felt solid.

'And the cat's much smaller than you.'

'Hmm,' said Sean, kneeling on all fours.

He held the torch in front of his face and lit up a small circle of books.

'Here kitty, kitty.'

'Em, you're hilarious. Which way was it facing?'

'To its left, I think.'

Sean cast the torch beam along the uppermost row of books. There were covers of red, green, black, brown, and blue, but there was nothing unusual. He scoured each row until eventually, something glistened.

'What's that?' said Emily.

'Where?' said Sean.

'Down a bit. To your left. There!'

The torch beam settled on a small, golden statue shaped like a seated elephant. It had four arms, a curved trunk and a halo above its head. A jewel in its belly glistened, and a bright green beam of light shone straight into Sean's eyes.

'Hey!' said Sean, turning away.

An instant later, the light went out.

'Are you okay?' said Emily.

Before Sean could reply, there was a loud rumble. A section of the bookshelf slid forwards. It scraped to one side and revealed a flight of steps.

'Bingo,' said Sean. 'Come on, we don't have much time.'

'After you,' said Emily.

Sean picked his way carefully down the steps. At their base was a narrow corridor lit by storm lamps. The walls were panelled in wood, with at least a dozen polished oak doors.

'Where's the cat?' said Emily.

Sean prodded his watch.

'It must be out of range.'

Emily tried a door handle. It was locked. She tried another, again without success.

'Great plan.'

'Keep trying,' said Sean. 'I'll take this side; you take the other.'

Each of the doors refused to budge, while ahead of them the corridor turned right and was blocked by a heavy fire-door.

'Last one,' said Emily.

She turned a brass handle, and to her surprise, it clicked open.

'Here we go,' whispered Sean.

Inside, was a windowless office that smelled of pepper and polish. Sean cast the torch beam around the room and gasped at what he saw.

'Woah!'

He clicked on the light switch.

'Oh no, the lights of doom!' said Emily.

The office was roughly square and arranged like a study. In front of an empty fireplace, lay a brightly patterned rug depicting animals and hunters in faded reds, oranges, and gold. Behind it, a leather-clad desk commanded the room. It was flanked by a pair of glass-fronted display cases; each crammed with gold and silver trinkets. On the other side was a long, wooden table.

'Just look at it all,' said Emily, crossing the rug.

The nearest case contained trays of brooches, bracelets, rings, and medallions. Each piece was decorated with intricate patterns and brightly coloured stones of every hue. Sean spotted beetles, cobras, and eagles among the collection.

'I think most of it's Egyptian.'

'There's an ankh cross,' said Emily. 'And look at this necklace, it's beautiful.'

The necklace was struck in gold and depicted a winged creature praying to a large painted eye that seemed to be crying a giant teardrop. Attached to the eye was an ornate collar of multi-coloured beads.

'I've seen this design somewhere before,' said Sean.

'It's the eye of Horus,' said Emily, brightly.

'Eye of Horace?' said Sean.

Emily tutted.

'No, silly, *Hor-us*, the ancient Egyptian god of the sky. It's meant to protect you from evil.'

Sean grinned.

'How?' It's in a glass case.'

'When you *wear* it,' said Emily, raising her eyebrows.

She approached a collection of photographs and brightly painted jars which were arranged on the table.

'Look at this photo, Sean.'

'Why? It's just a man in uniform, stood next to another man in uniform.'

'Take a closer look.'

Sean stared blankly at the photograph.

'Don't you get it? It's Major Clavity when he was younger.'

Sean felt tears gather in the corners of his eyes.

'What's the matter?' said Emily.

He raised a finger and touched the glass in front of the second figure.

'And this… is Dad.'

'Are you sure?'

'We had a picture just like this at home.'

Sean felt the warmth of Emily's hand on his shoulder.

'I think we should have a chat with Major Clavity, don't you?'

Sean let out a sigh. If only it was that easy.

Behind them, the door rattled, and Sean noticed a shadow enter the room. It leapt onto the table and brushed against a jar, making it wobble.

'Crash!'

'Aren't we having a smashing time?' said the cat. 'You two are in *so* much trouble.'

'You broke that!' said Emily. 'You wretched creature.'

'I prefer biobot,' said the cat. 'It's more accurate.'

'You blundering, bilge rat,' said Emily.

Sean knelt and sifted through the debris. His stomach was in knots. He picked up a large piece of painted earthenware and noticed a faded brown tube lying underneath it.

'What is it?' said Emily.

'I don't know.'

Sean lifted the tube and felt a small, oval object drop into his lap. He unrolled the tube.

'I think it's a scroll.'

'What does it say?' said Emily.

Sean felt the scroll crackle between his fingers. It was ridged and covered in rows of painted symbols.

'It's written in pictures,' said Sean, turning his watch to face the symbols.

'Hieroglyphs?' said Emily. 'It must be Egyptian.'

The cat stepped forward.

'My scanners indicate the papyrus you are holding is thousands of years old. Your fingers are covering it in sweat, Sean.'

'Then what's it doing here?' said Emily.

'What's what doing here?' said a loud voice from the doorway.

Sean looked up in horror and saw Hughes holding a torch and sidearm. Hughes glanced at the broken vase and glowered at them.

'You are both grounded. No amount of glue is going to fix that.'

'But we…' said Emily.

'I suppose you wandered into the Founder's study while

you were sleepwalking? Despite the fact it's locked inside a restricted area?'

Sean and Emily shrugged.

'I have a good mind to put you both in the cells. Out! Now!'

Sean slipped the oval object into his dressing gown pocket and followed Emily to the corridor.

'I trust you have an explanation for your actions?' said Hughes.

'Actually, we do,' said Sean. 'Shall we wake up our mums and Mr Brawne?'

Hughes stopped in his tracks.

'Are you serious?'

'Yes. And I'm sure Mum would like to know why our shoes have been bugged.'

'And why your robotic cat has been spying on us?' said Emily.

Hughes fell silent for a moment.

'Look, why don't we talk it over in the morning?'

Sean smiled.

'And perhaps the Founder should join us?'

Hughes frowned.

'Don't push your luck, mate. My cells are just itching for some new customers.'

Emily put on her angelic face.

'Fine, we'll go back to our bedrooms. Won't we, Sean?'

'I believe you are overlooking a priceless vase, which is now smashed into several hundred pieces?' said the cat, sauntering behind them.

'Which *you* broke,' said Emily.

Hughes turned to the cat.

'Is that true, BC135?'

The cat flicked its tail and strolled past.

'I was protecting a restricted area from intruders.'

'BC135, report to Security immediately for debriefing,' said Hughes.

'If you insist,' said the cat.

'I *do* insist,' said Hughes. 'And if I ever catch you two in here again…'

Sean stood beside Emily and gave a cheesy smile.

'Just go! Before I change my mind.'

Sean and Emily half walked and half ran back to the library.

'Told you so,' said Sean.

Emily smiled.

'And I suppose you knew this would happen all along?'

'Sort of.'

'Liar,' said Emily with a smile. 'And what do you think Hughes will do now?'

'Blame the cat?'

Emily laughed.

'If we're lucky, they might even melt it down.'

'Fat chance,' said Sean. 'Besides…no cat, no prize.'

'Huh?' said Emily, with a quizzical look.

Sean dipped his hand into his dressing gown pocket and produced a smooth, black pebble.

'The crystal?' said Emily, with her eyes wide.

Sean Yeager Adventures – the story so far

Welcome to the world of Sean Yeager Adventures. Here's a quick run-down of what to expect from the rest of the stories in the series. As well as spies, gadgets, robots, aliens and action, there's a plot that runs from episode to episode.

In the DNA Thief, Sean Yeager's life is interrupted by a burglary that leads to a hair-raising attempt to recover his lost belongings. Sean is introduced to the Foundation and a world he knew nothing about. For some reason, Sean's DNA is the prize.

In Hunters Hunted, as you have just read, Sean meets Emily Campbell at a country safe house. Together, they investigate the mansion and find clues to a mysterious treasure and their fathers. Meanwhile, enemy forces close in and cause mayhem.

In Claws of Time, the wheels fall off the Foundation's operation. Sean and Emily embark on a mission to save Major Clavity and encounter far more than they bargained for. Across the world, satellites are crashing and the clues lead to Darius Deveraux. Meanwhile, Vex has his hands full with a vengeful sentient.

In Mortal Thread, Sean and Emily must find a way to save the Founder. However, the Foundation is divided and Deveraux's forces have seized the initiative. Agent Stafford is assigned the mission he has long dreaded, while Sean and Emily search for the Wanderer and seek help from the US.

Sean Yeager Adventures – frequently asked questions

Q: Why do you write the Sean Yeager stories from multiple perspectives?

To keep the stories fast moving and to show more of the characters. From the feedback we've received, most readers enjoy seeing the bad guys and the good guys in action. We also seek to write movies on the page, because it keeps things fresh and different.

Q: Is Brigadier Cuthbertson a reference to Dr Who and are you influenced by the Dr Who series?

Not really, no. The Brigadier is an affectionate nod to Dr Who, which we have watched over the years. It is also a well-established military rank in the UK. However, the Brigadier is far from the focus of the stories as becomes clear during the series. Much as we enjoy Dr Who, SYA does not feature time travel or daleks.

Q: Why is Deveraux so evil?

Darius Deveraux's character has been shaped by his ambitions and his master. As you read the series it will become clear why he behaves the way he does. Without giving away too much from later books, let's just say he's not evil just for the sake of it.

Q: Why are Sean and Emily's families living together at Kimbleton Hall?

Because they have a lot in common, including their guardians. As the series progresses it becomes clear why Sean and Emily are looked after by the Foundation.

Q: Who is your favourite character to write?
It is currently a tie between Dr Vex and a new character KB. Darius Deveraux is also fun to work with, at a safe distance.

Q: What is the Foundation and what are they doing?
The Foundation for International Technology is run by the Founder - Cassius Olandis - and others. As the series progresses their origins and mission are explained. They have been around for quite a long time.

Q: Did you work out the back story and answers to the SYA mysteries before you wrote the books? And does the reader find out answers about everything that's going on?
Yes, pretty much. We work out a lot of back story before starting each book and in fact before even starting the series. Rather than 'telling' everything up front, we invite the reader to figure things out for themselves, to guess what is happening and discover answers as the series progresses. All the big questions *are* answered in the series that is a promise! However, all is not as it seems. There is a substantial back story and 'expanded universe' yet to be written in book form, which may emerge in prequels in future.

Q: What happened to Sean's father?
During the series this becomes clear. It is covered in the later episodes.

Q: What happened in Egypt?
Let's just say, the Founder and his colleagues have been around for quite a while. Check out the history of Pharaoh Akhenaton.

Thank you for your interest in Sean Yeager Adventures.

We publish news and updates from time to time on the Sean Yeager WordPress blog and at:

www.SeanYeager.com

Please support SYA by posting a review on Amazon or Goodreads if you (or your child) enjoys a Sean Yeager book. All reviews are much appreciated and they really help to spread the word to other readers (and parents). We also read reviews to go back and improve earlier books - DNA Thief and Hunters Hunted have both been updated extensively based on feedback from readers.

CPSIA information can be obtained
at www.ICGtesting.com
Printed in the USA
LVHW010959290122
709475LV00010B/1325